DON'T PLAY WIT' A *Boss*

A NORTH MIAMI LOVE STORY

A Novel By

KAI'OR ELLE

© 2019 Royalty Publishing House

Published by Royalty Publishing House
www.royaltypublishinghouse.com

ALL RIGHTS RESERVED

Any unauthorized reprint or use of the material is prohibited. No part of this book may be reproduced or transmitted in any form or by any means, electronic or mechanical, including photocopying, recording, or by any information storage without express permission by the author or publisher. This is an original work of fiction. Names, characters, places and incidents are either products of the author's imagination or are used fictitiously and any resemblance to actual persons, living or dead, is entirely coincidental.

Contains explicit language & adult themes suitable for ages 16+ only.

Royalty Publishing House is now accepting manuscripts from aspiring or experienced urban romance authors!

WHAT MAY PLACE YOU ABOVE THE REST:

Heroes who are the ultimate book bae: strong-willed, maybe a little rough around the edges but willing to risk it all for the woman he loves.

Heroines who are the ultimate match: the girl next door type, not perfect - has her faults but is still a decent person. One who is willing to risk it all for the man she loves.

The rest is up to you! Just be creative, think out of the box, keep it sexy and intriguing!

If you'd like to join the Royal family, send us the first 15K words (60 pages) of your completed manuscript to submissions@royaltypublishing-house.com

Synopsis

Real bosses always get what they want. No matter if it's money, the woman of their dreams, or even revenge. The best thing to do when it comes to them is stay out of their way and never ever play with their hearts, because things can get ugly.

When Cadence finds herself in a situation that leads straight to murder with no alibi she flees to a new town to be surrounded by new faces. The last thing she is searching for is love but what is she to do when it comes searching for her? Her past may be murky, but this is one kill she isn't going to want to miss or run from.

Killian better known as "Kill" in the rugged streets of North Miami is the definition of a self-made boss. When tragedy strikes and leaves him cold to the core he never expects to be the same again. That is until he crosses paths with Cadence. His heart is cold, and trust isn't something he's willing to give, but something about her just may change everything. Will Cadence attempt to play with a boss or will her love be real from the start?

Tehani

"Nigga, the fuck did I just say?" I looked down and barked at the fine ass nigga that was in between my legs.

My thighs may have been juicy, and my legs may have been locked around his head, but I knew for a fact that none of that was interfering with his hearing. His ass heard me loud and clear when I told him to keep eating this pussy because he had stopped like he thought he was about to slide into my honey pot. That was never a part of the plan and he knew that before he brought his ass over here, so why he even tried was beyond me.

"Ain't no stopping, baby. Don't even try that shit right now," he mumbled right before shoving his face back into my wetness.

"I said move, jackass!" I slapped his ass in the head and unlocked my legs. He immediately sat up and started to look at me stupid, but I didn't give a fuck. My phone was ringing, and it wasn't a phone call I could miss if it was who I thought it was. "You can go now," I said as soon as I confirmed that the call was indeed who I thought it was from.

"Really, Tee? You gone kick me out for some jail dick that you can't even get right now?"

"Bye, Jaydon!" I rolled my eyes hard as shit at him before quickly answering the call. My boo ain't like to wait and he would hang up if I

1

took too long to answer. Jaydon was just gone have to kiss my fat ass and cash his feelings elsewhere because those bitches sure as hell wasn't about to get cashed by me. "Hey, baby." I cooed into the phone as soon as I heard my man's voice. He may have been in prison, but that didn't stop him from calling whenever he felt like it. He had got a cellphone his first week in there and the pigs had yet to catch him with it.

Jay stood in the middle of my floor looking hurt. He was pissing me off because he knew how this shit went. Hell, this was like the millionth time this shit had happened and interrupted his pussy eating session. There would be other mornings. He didn't even have to worry about that, but he was going to have to worry about it if his ass didn't leave my house. I walked out of the room he was in so I could talk to my nigga in peace.

"You heard me?" Keef asked on the other end of the phone.

"No, what did you say?"

"I said why the fuck you sound all out of breath at five in the damn morning?"

"What is you saying? You know I had to hop up quick as fuck when I heard my phone ringing. Now, I'm walking to the bathroom to start my water for a bath." Hey, at least nothing I had said was a lie. I did have to hop the fuck up and I was walking in the bathroom to run my water as we spoke.

"You right, I'm tripping. I'm calling because that nigga Kill got a problem with the crate of guns you sold to him last week."

"When the fuck doesn't Kill have a problem? If he doesn't like the way we do business then he needs to take his money AND business somewhere else."

"Ay, shut the fuck up talking like that, girl. See, you about to piss me off good and early this morning. I can just feel it. That nigga brings in the most money for our business, so no the fuck he can't take his money or business elsewhere. Now, I already talked to him and he's on the way over there now."

"Now?" I frantically asked.

"Yeah, now, what the hell wrong with you?"

"Nothing, it's just early as fuck. So, what exactly is his problem?" I questioned as I practically sprinted to the living room. It was a good thing I did too because right when Jaydon was about to open the door someone was knocking on it. He looked at me like *what the fuck?* as I pulled him by his arm to the back door and shoved his lanky ass out of it.

"He says the guns you gave him ain't new when he specifically asked for new guns. So that's a fuck up on your end, Tehani."

"I know," I admitted. I had been so busy trying to keep up with my life, my relationship with Keef, and our gun business that shit often slipped my mind. If it didn't slip my mind I probably got it mixed up with something else. "Who is it?" I finally asked after I made my way back to the front door.

"Kill!" I heard a voice roar from the other side of the door. I rolled my eyes before I opened the door.

"What, bruh, damn?" I quizzed.

"I ain't yo' fucking bruh and say my name when you talking to me. I don't know if you woke up stupid or what but I ain't yo' nigga. Therefore, I ain't got to deal with all that slick shit you popping right now."

"I guess, Destiny's Child." I huffed. "Babe, let me deal with this motherfucker and his situation," I said into the phone.

"Ay, put a smile on yo' face. I know you probably looking mean as fuck right now. Just remember it's all about the bag. Secure that motherfucker and have a good day. I'll hit you back later on. They rounding us up to go eat breakfast now. Love you, bye."

"Love you too." I hung up the phone and looked back up at Kill. "What can I help you with, Kill?"

"You can help me with getting another fucking crate and not one with used guns. I know you already know that, so before we get to that, answer this for me."

"What?"

"Why the fuck is there a pregnant person asleep on your porch?"

"A who?" I asked, stepping out of the house. When I did I saw a pregnant girl on my porch swing knocked out. "What the fuck?"

Cadence

"Excuse me," I heard someone say before poking at my leg.

My eyes popped open and that's when I remembered where I was at. I pulled my hair out of my face and sat up slowly on the porch swing I had fallen asleep on. I wasn't in my home state anymore. I wasn't even on the west coast anymore. I was on the east coast and I could tell a huge difference, but I wasn't complaining. I couldn't after the little situation I had ran away from back home, but I'll be keeping that story to myself for now. You just didn't know who you could trust these days and I couldn't have that information getting into the wrong hands.

"Tehani?" I looked up and asked the girl that had been poking me. It definitely looked like her, but I wanted to make sure.

"Cadence? Girl, is that you?"

"Yes."

"Oh my god, what are you doing here? I haven't seen you since you were like eleven and I was twelve!"

"Surprise," I said with an uneasy smile.

Tehani and I were childhood best friends. We used to do everything together and we used to get into a lot of trouble together too. I was the nice one while Tehani was the naughty one. The girl couldn't hold her tongue even if she was paid to do so. Whatever she thought just had to come out. She had always been wild while I chose the more careful way to do things. After what I had done I may just be on the wild side now too. I had no choice though and I was only protecting myself.

"The best surprise ever! I been telling you for years to come out here and see me ever since we found each other on Facebook and you just shot my hopes down every time."

"Well, I'm here now." I stood up and stretched. I knew I was eventually going to have to tell Tehani what I was really doing here, but for now I would just allow her to think that I was visiting.

"Well, I'm glad y'all got that shit solved. Now back to my fucking crate," I heard someone say in a deep gritty voice.

I looked over and saw the most handsome man I had ever laid eyes on. His skin was light brown and his eyes were slanted and very dark. His hair was braided down to the sides of his head with a long part going down the middle. Before I saw him I always felt like after a certain age braids weren't for guys. I'll admit that he made them look sexy though.

I could tell that tattoos were his thing because he was covered in them. He even had a girl's name and some date tatted right above his eyebrow off to the side. Tattoos on the face was a turnoff for me too, but just like the braids, he made it look sexy. I heard someone clear their throat and I awkwardly pulled my eyes off of the handsome stranger.

"Cadence, you good?" Tehani inquired.

"You say what now?" I looked up at her and asked. I was sure that I looked like a complete idiot.

"Is everything okay with you?"

"Why you ask that?" I placed my hands on my stomach out of habit.

"Well, you just zoned out on me and I did kind of find you on my porch asleep. Oh, and you pregnant," Tehani explained, clicking her tongue at the end.

"Back to my crates. Y'all gone have to get to all of that later," the stranger blurted out.

When I dared to look at him again I saw that he was looking right at me. I wanted to look away, but his stare was so intense that I couldn't. His eyes told his story for him. He was a rough guy and I could only imagine the type of things that he had seen. Something inside of me wanted to hold him and let him know that it was okay to let go of whatever it was that he was holding on to. The hurt in his eyes was indescribable, and I wanted badly to take that hurt away.

It was crazy to want to save a stranger as bad as I wanted to save him. The truth was, I needed saving myself and the little hope inside of me was hoping that if I saved someone, maybe someone would come and save me as well. At this point, I wouldn't be able to save myself and that's why I had ran to start with.

"Cady, come on in and make yourself at home. I'll show you were you can sleep and things after I take care of him. Come on, Kill." We all walked inside, and I sat down in the living room while Tehani disappeared down the hallway with the guy named Kill. *Now what in the hell kind of name was that?*

Killian

"Do you have the other crate with you?" Tehani questioned as she led me down the basement stairs.

"No, why?" I asked, irritated.

"What you mean, no why?" She smacked her teeth and stopped at the bottom of the stairs.

"That's a stupid ass question. Why the fuck would I have the crate with used guns in it with me? We both know them fucking guns dirty, so why would I ride around with that shit in my car?"

"Uhm, because you making an exchange."

"And who the fuck told you that lie?"

"Didn't you say you wanted new guns?"

"I do, but you ain't getting them other guns back. That means it ain't no exchange."

"You got to pay way more money for these new guns than you did for them dirty ones. You do know that right?"

"What kind of nigga do you take me for? I pay for everything. I ain't never been the type to take or expect a handout. That's your problem now, you talk too fucking much, Tehani. Keef gotta' know that shit is bad for business, but I mind my own damn business. If I didn't, I would talk about why Jaydon was slipping out of yo' back door. You see Keef don't work for me, but Jaydon do. Keep that shit in mind with yo' messy ass. Now where the fuck this crate at so I can get the fuck up out of here."

"Follow me," Tehani said with a lot of attitude. I didn't give a shit about her attitude. I had important things to deal with and her attitude ain't make the list.

"This it?" I asked after she had stopped in front of a shelf built into the wall.

"Yeah, this all the new shit on this shelf. This crate right here has the best shit in it, that's why I'm showing it to you. The lord knows I don't want to see your fucking face anytime soon." She had mumbled the last part, but I still heard her ass. I just smirked at her.

"I'll take it. Here you go." I shoved a wad of cash into her hands.

"Hold up, I ain't tell you how much it was yet."

"Yeah, keep the change." I grabbed the crate off of the shelf and turned around to walk towards the stairs. When I got to the first step I stopped and turned back around to say something. "You might want to invest in some security. It ain't safe to have the motherfuckers buying from you coming down here where you have everything stashed at. You could sell to the wrong person and get knocked over yo' damn head. Anyway, the girl upstairs... what's up with her?"

"Really, Kill? You said all of that to ask about Cadence? Don't worry about me though, I stay ready to fuck a nigga up." Tehani reached behind her back and revealed a pink Glock.

"That ain't gone do shit." I waved her off. "Cadence... I like that name. Don't worry about telling me shit. I'm about to go find out for myself. I don't need yo' messy ass in the middle of shit I'm interested in."

"What does that supposed to mean, Kill!" she yelled to my back because I was already headed back up the stairs.

Cadence

I was sitting on the couch in the living room waiting for Tehani to come back. There was only one word to describe Tehani's style. Colorful. The couch I was sitting on was powder blue and so was the other couch. She had a love seat that was bright yellow and a recliner that was dark orange. The curtains were bubble gum pink and the carpet was violet. It was a sight to see and all of the colors was starting to make me nauseous.

Tehani was black and Hawaiian. Her hair was thick and black, and it came down to her bra straps. She was slightly on the thick side with just enough of everything. She always had a body to die for and from the look of things that hadn't changed. I on the other hand had changed a lot. I was once slim thick, but the baby wasn't playing with my butt. I'd packed on a few healthy pounds and my stomach was sticking out like I was eight months when I was really only five.

The baby had given my warm chocolate skin a delightful glow that I couldn't deny. Even when I felt like shit I still looked magical. It was truly a gift and a curse because no one knew when I wasn't in the mood to be bothered. Lately, I'd just adapted to smiling, even when it was the last thing I wanted to do.

"How many months are you?" a deep voice asked, startling me.

DON'T PLAY WIT' A BOSS: A NORTH MIAMI LOVE STORY

"Excuse me?"

"You hard of hearing?"

"No."

"You sure?"

"I'm sure."

"I said, how many months are you?"

"Oh, I'm five months." I said it more to the floor than I did to him. I was trying my best not to look up at him. I didn't want to get caught up in his storytelling eyes again.

"I'm up here."

"I had something on my shoes," I said, quickly.

"You got something on yo' tongue too. It's called a lie, but I'll let it slide. Can I take you out sometime?" he had the audacity to ask. I couldn't help but to snort because I found that very funny.

"You want to take a pregnant chick out? Either I'm crazy or you're just that desperate and I know for a fact that I'm not crazy."

"Wow."

"Wow what?" I asked getting offended.

"It's been that long since someone asked you out?" he boldly questioned.

"What's going on in here?" Tehani finally walked back into the living room and asked. She walked over to me and passed me a bottle of water.

"Your friend was just leaving. That's what's going on."

"Girl, he ain't no friend of mine. Just somebody I do business with that's all. I don't know why he came up here bothering you anyway. You not like these thirsty hoes around here, I'm sure. That money don't impress nobody, Kill."

"I ain't said shit about no money. I move different. I'll get up with you later, Cadence." And just like that he was gone.

"Close your mouth, girl. Dang, you feeling him, huh?"

"Who me? Oh, nooo nooo no! You ain't changed a bit, Tee. I see that look on your face. You're cooking up something in your head that ain't even going on. Trust me, love is the last thing my pregnant ass is looking for right now."

"Bitch, don't nobody give a shit about you being pregnant. That don't mean shit this day and age. Yo ass been on the farm way too long." Tehani laughed.

"Stop lying! I haven't even seen a farm up close before. You know how my people is. It's all about the ocean life with them back in California."

"Girl, when I first had to move away when I was twelve all I did was dream about the ocean life. I still can't believe the courts turned me over to my crack fiend mother over my daddy. I went straight from California to down here in north Miami. Don't get me wrong, the oceans here are beautiful, but my life ain't no pretty picture. I practically had to raise myself. My mother only cleaned up long enough to get me back so she could receive those state checks for me. The system so fucked up that they allowed that shit to happen too."

"Damn, Tehani, I didn't know that."

"Shit, no one did."

"Why didn't you just come back to California?"

"Girl, with what money? I was a kid, remember?"

"Well, you could have told someone."

"And got taken by the state? They sure as hell wasn't about to send me back to my father. He was dating that nineteen-year-old girl at the time and that shit was frowned upon by everybody. The whole thing was real fucked up, but I survived."

"I can see that, Tee, you look beautiful."

"And so do you, boo! This shit right here is so unreal right now. Who would have ever thought that I would link back up with my childhood best friend?"

"Definitely not me, but I'm glad I came."

"Which brings us back to why were you asleep on my porch?"

"Girl, I tried to knock on the door, but no one ever came. I knew for a fact this was the address you sent so I decided to wait on the swing. I must have fallen asleep while waiting."

"Bitch, this is North Miami. Don't do that shit no more, fuck around and get shot."

"You so silly." I laughed.

"No, I'm so serious. Now, come on so I can show you the guestroom."

"Wait, before we do that, what's up with that guy?" I heard myself ask. I hadn't meant to, but it just slipped out and the lord knew I was dying to find out.

"He a certified boss, there's no denying that. He's just real arrogant. It's like he thinks he knows everything, and that shit can get annoying. He comes with baggage though."

"I knew it was something!"

"Nah, nothing like that. It's some real crazy shit though. His baby mama drowned their two-year-old daughter in the bathtub a little over a year ago. It was all over the news."

"Oh my god are you serious? I was just so rude to him." I gasped.

"Don't trip. He likes to pretend like it didn't happen, so never bring it up. If I was him I would probably try to act like it didn't happen too, but we both know that it wouldn't take the pain away."

"Right," I said, quickly getting lost in my own thoughts.

That was it. That's the story that his mesmerizing eyes were telling. I felt so bad for him and I wanted to be his comfort even more than before. That would probably never happen though since I had been so mean to him. It's not like I could honestly jump into anything right now anyway. No matter what happened here, there was still a situation back home that was unresolved, and I only prayed that it stayed that way.

Killian

I was speeding down the fast lane trying to get back home when my phone started ringing. I picked it up out the seat beside me and looked down at the number. I sucked my teeth and threw the phone back on the passenger side seat. I put on my signal light as I eased into the other lane to make a right turn. There really was no need for me to be speeding, but it was a bad habit of mine.

I was already expecting Jaydon to be late since I had seen him walking out of Tehani's backyard. I didn't understand why he wanted to fuck around with that girl when he already had a chick at home. Not only did he have a chick at home, but she was helping him raise his bad ass sister who was too grown just to be a teenager. It took patience and a lot of loyalty to voluntarily deal with Jaydon's sister. Their mother had been sick in the hospital for a few months and he had been watching after his sister ever since. Yet, that didn't stop him from his dog ways. To each his own, but I didn't get down like that.

I didn't see the thrill in entertaining a lot of women at once. I preferred to settle down with one woman and cater to that woman only. Doing exactly that had led me right into misery. Being the right man for the wrong woman was my first mistake. Now, here it was over a year later, and I was still suffering from heartache. I was still accusing myself for a situation that wasn't my fault. I know that, but I felt like if I had done just one thing different I wouldn't be in the situation that I was in today. I had just turned into my yard when my phone started ringing again. I snatched it up from the seat and quickly answered it out of anger that I just couldn't let go of.

"Yeah, I accept the fucking charges," I barked into the phone and a few seconds later I was connected with my caller from the county jail.

"You answered for me," a soft voice, that I once loved the sound of, said.

"I answered to tell you to stop fucking calling me!"

"Kill, can you just hear me out?"

"Hear you out for what, Tyra? It ain't shit for me and you to be discussing."

"How can you say that when we have a child together?"

"HAD, we had a child together before your evil ass did what the fuck you did. You cheated on me and got caught. I had every right to leave you because of that but you didn't have the right to take my fucking child's life just because I wouldn't take you back!" A tear escaped, and I quickly wiped it away. Only one thing could make a grown ass boss like me cry, and that one thing was my now deceased two-year-old daughter.

"I told you and the court I wasn't in my right mind when everything happened. I should be getting mental help, instead I'm in here. These people are going to kill me in here. You have to do something. I don't deserve this type of life! I'm not a murderer! I wasn't in my right mind. You have to believe me, Kill. Or no one else will!"

"You can rot in fucking hell and you can save that bullshit about your mind not being in the right place. What could possibly just snap in your mind and make you decide *'I'm going to kill my two-year-old daughter today?'* Not a damn thing can justify that shit. Fuck you, bitch! You lucky to be where you are right now and that's all I'll say on that." I hung up the phone and took a deep breath.

I shouldn't have even answered her call. Now I was pissed the fuck off and my heart was hurting. I couldn't cry anymore though. That wouldn't bring my daughter back, nothing would or could. Her name was Kiari and I had gotten her name and birth date tatted above my eye. It couldn't heal the pain, but it definitely made me smile whenever I looked in the mirror and saw her name. I got out of my car, slammed the door shut, and then made my way inside of my home.

I walked straight through my mansion until I had reached the back glass-door. I opened the door and walked out so I could sit on my patio and smoke a blunt. It was still early, so I had time to get my mind right before my people started pulling up for the meeting. I reached over and pulled a drawer out of the outdoor dresser I had sitting right by my chair. I kept at least ten blunts rolled at a time and stashed in there for days just like this one. I pulled one out and lit it with my lighter. I instantly felt myself relax and before I knew it my mind had drifted back to the pregnant girl that was at Tehani's house.

Something was up with her. She was too damn nervous to only be visiting a friend. Plus, she didn't even have many bags with her. I always thought when women went out of town they overpacked, but she looked like she had under packed. None of that was my business, I just couldn't get her angelic face out of my mind. Pregnancy looked nice on her. I didn't know if that was what was attracting me to her or what, but either way I felt like I had to find out more about her.

Deep down inside I was hurt, and I knew that I could never have Kiari back. That didn't mean that I couldn't have more children or play the father to another child. I stopped myself right after that thought had escaped. Here I was ready to play stepdaddy to a baby who hadn't even been born yet with a woman I hardly even knew. The shit was insane.

I decided right then that the best thing for me to do was probably stay as far away from Cadence as possible. A woman like that couldn't possibly handle all the baggage that a nigga like me came with. The lifestyle I lived was for a true boss only. Half these niggas out here couldn't walk a mile in my shoes, and I didn't even want to put her anywhere near the lifestyle I was living, but if things were just a little different, she would be mine for sure.

Jaydon

"I used my brother's money. Money ain't shit to him. He got it, always gone get it, and always gone have it—" I heard my little sister Jayohna quoting my motto as I swaggered in the kitchen. I quickly jumped in to finish her sentence.

"Cause it ain't shit to get to the paper route!"

"See, that's where she gets that shit from," my girlfriend Madden said as she grabbed some orange juice out of the fridge. I looked over at the table and saw that she had cooked us a whole meal for breakfast.

"What happened now?" I quizzed with a smirk.

"Tell your brother what you did, Jayohna."

"What you do, baby girl? Oh, look at you. Yo hair look straight for real, sis. You just got that done?" I questioned, getting off track.

"Yep, sure did. You know Wesley right?" Jayohna asked, looking at me.

"Yeah Wes, that lil' nigga that stay posted on the block, right?"

"That's right. His mama was the one that did my hair."

"Word?"

"Yep."

"And she took out the goddess braids I had just paid for. She used the money she gets from you to get a sew-in instead. That's what she forgot to mention," Madden said.

"That's what you fussing about, Madden? Chill out, she straight. I'll put the money back in your account after I go and holler at Kill in a lil' bit. I'm about to eat right fast and then head right back out after I get out the shower."

"Holler at Kill? Get out the shower? All I'm hearing right now is that you've been out fucking around on me. Now, I dare you to look me in my eyes and tell me that I'm lying." She walked over and stopped right in front of me.

"Dumb ass girl. Well, that's my cue to get out of here. I have a ride to school. I'll get up with y'all later," Jayohna tried to mumble the first part before saying everything else clearly. I just ignored her calling Madden dumb. Jayohna tended to say whatever was on her mind, she just couldn't help it.

"Cool, here take this band. Did you already eat, or you gone stop on the way to school and get something?" I asked as I passed her a wad of cash.

"I'mma get something on the way. Love you, big bruh. I'm out." Jayohna took off out the kitchen and a few seconds later I heard the front door open and close.

"Can I get an answer now?" Madden asked, annoyed.

"What you talking about, Madden? Ain't nobody been out fucking off on yo' sexy ass. I mean look at you, baby. You the color of some golden grahams, you got a nice petite body, you not too short or too tall, but you just the height I like em'. Look at them thick ass lips and them beautiful eyes. I'll be a damn fool to fuck around on you." I ran a hand through her straight black hair. She loved when I would do that shit. She cracked a smile at me, and I knew I was off the hook for this morning. No matter what I did Madden always forgave me and I had grown accustomed to it. "There go that million-dollar smile."

"Shut up! You the one with the million-dollar smile with all those damn diamonds and shit in ya mouth."

"Don't be mad cause you can't walk around with diamonds in ya grill like me."

"Whatever, let's sit down and eat. I ain't cook all this food for nothing." She grabbed my hand and pulled me over to the table.

I enjoyed a quick meal with her and then I rushed to take my shower. After I got out of the shower I jumped fresh with a new outfit and put a little jewelry on before heading out of the bedroom. Madden was in the living room watching TV now. I walked over to where she was sitting and leaned down to give her a kiss. She kissed me back and looked at me.

I could see the hurt all in her eyes because she knew for a fact that I was fucking off on her again. I didn't have time to coddle her though so I pecked her lips one more time and told her that I would see her later before heading out and going to get in my car. I started the engine and got on the road, happy to be back out of the house with her so I could call Tehani. I pulled my phone out and did just that as I drove.

"What's up, baby? What took you so long to answer?" I asked as soon as she said hello.

I didn't know what it was about Tehani, but she had it. She was sexy as a motherfucker, but my girl was sexy too, so that wasn't what it was. If I had to be honest I think it was her seducing ass ways that got to me. That damn girl would get me over to her place and make her move on me after teasing me in all kind of different ways. Then, when we would get to the bedroom she'd put her sweet ass pussy right in my mouth.

It was over after she'd done that. She tasted like fucking coconuts and pineapples; I swear to god. It was like drinking the last cup of your favorite juice, you never wanted that shit to end man. She knew she had that nectar too. That's why she was out here in the streets doing whatever the fuck she wanted to do.

Her nigga was behind them walls and he wasn't stopping shit that was going on, on the outside. I didn't know if the nigga was truly blind to the type of bitch he had or if he was just playing stupid. Whatever it was it seemed to be working for them, but that's where I came into the picture. I wanted Tehani for my fucking self and I planned to make it happen slowly but surely. The difference between me and Keef was, I actually knew what the fuck was going on and I planned to put a stop to it.

Of course, I wouldn't be leaving Madden because she was mine for life with no wedding ring. I just couldn't let her go. She took care of home and I needed that in my life. Tehani was too wild to play the home role, but she would be perfect for the side chick role. I don't mean just any side chick either. I mean a loyal side chick. If you could find you one of those or turn a bitch into one of those, you were straight. Aside from chasing money that was the mission I was on out here and that was just the way it had to be. A fly nigga like me was never meant for just one bitch.

"I think you dialed the wrong number, Jaydon," I heard Tehani snap on the other end of the line.

"Nah, this the right fucking number!"

"Nuh uh, see it can't be. For one, you ain't behind them walls. Two, yo' name ain't Keef and three, you don't put no money in these pockets. I call you over when I want my pussy licked on and that's it. Ain't shit else popping this way, bruh. Oh, and I don't appreciate the way you were carrying on this morning eitha'. You already know when my nigga call you got to get the fuck out. I don't give a damn how good this pussy tasting to you. Oh, and another damn thing, since when the fuck did you think it was cool for you to slide up in this. Don't try that shit no more, nigga. Now have a nice fucking day and you'll hear from me IF you are needed again."

"Did this motherfucker just hang up on me?" I asked out loud and quickly looked down at the phone. She had definitely hung up on me.

You see, it was the shit like that, that made me crave her sexy ass. I felt my dick brick up and I wanted to make a detour to her house, so she could let me feel her mouth. She never wanted to do that either. Matter fact, the only thing Tehani ever wanted was her pussy ate and that shit was okay with me. I was going to get that pussy and when I did I was gone fuck her world all up.

I finally pulled up to Kill's mansion and parked my car. I hopped out, hit the lock on my keychain and then made my way around the back. I already knew his ass would be on the patio smoking blunt after blunt. He wouldn't be Kill if he wasn't. I turned the corner and the first thing I saw was Kill posted up, smoking a blunt. My motherfucking nigga!

"Pass that shit." I walked up on the patio and slapped hands with Kill. He took one last pull from the blunt before passing it over to me.

"You earlier than I expected." Kill laughed

"Man, you say that bullshit every time. I told you the last time that Madden don't run shit. Jaydon runs the show because Jaydon makes the money and Jaydon keeps money in her accounts. Ya feel me, dawg?"

"Nigga, you fucking stupid. What the hell was yo' ass doing slipping out of Tehani's crib this morning?"

"You hitting that too?" I asked, eyebrow cocked like a motherfucker.

"Fuck no! Man, don't ask me no shit like that. I love down to earth women and she far from that shit. You already know how I move." Kill mean mugged me and I knew the nigga was offended by me asking him that.

"Ahhhhh! Yo serious ass, chill out. I'm just fucking with you, damn. Nah, but I'm trying to make that bitch my loyal side chick." I started smiling big, exposing my expensive permanent diamond grill.

"You an ugly motherfucker, nigga! You need to leave that motherfucker alone. As soon as word get back to Keef I already know we gone have a war on our hands. That's gone be stupid as shit because they who we get our guns from for the low. You know me though; I'll handle any situation that needs to be handled."

"Straight the fuck up." I slapped hands with Kill again.

That's exactly why he was my best friend. He'd tell you some shit that you needed to hear, and you knew was true. At the same time, he was down for whatever in the end. That's just how my dawg moved. Kill was twenty-nine and I was twenty-six. We didn't hang out much back in the day, but once real nigga's link up it's over after that.

"These other niggas should be pulling up right about now," Kill said, looking down at his watch. At that exact moment we could hear a couple of vehicles pulling up out front.

"I don't know how you do that shit."

"Do what?"

"Exactly what you just did, nigga. You said they should be pulling up and now the motherfuckers pulling up."

"Nah, I just know they know exactly how late they can be. Which in reality they not really late. I just say that shit because they don't know that I always tell them thirty minutes earlier than I actually want them to be here."

"This nigga, swear he got it all figured out."

"I do! Now let's get this meeting started so we can figure out how to wash all this dirty fucking money that keep coming in. I'm thinking about opening up a hotel franchise or a club or some shit. At this point we are bringing in way too much money without enough businesses to cover the shit."

"Nigga, what you mean? You already got over 10 businesses that's bringing in more than enough money."

"See, Jay, you not listening to me right now. I told you about doing that shit. Pay attention, nigga. Always pay attention. What the fuck I said was, I need to open more businesses to wash all of this dirty ass drug money that keep rolling in. I'm not opening the businesses to make money, although that is a plus, but I'm opening them to wash all of this dirty money. These people see a nigga like me getting money and their minds get to wondering. Once their minds get to wondering they're on you like white on rice and yo' black ass better have some answers for them. If you don't you going to fucking jail and I'd bet my last dollar on that shit. The key is to play it smart and stay one step ahead of them because if they catch you, anything is liable to happen."

"What the fuck y'all nigga's talking about around here?" Boston asked walking up on the patio with two other niggas that we fucked with.

"We talking about yo' slow ass holding up the meeting, nigga," Kill joked.

"Shit, I just knew I was on time. You ain't slick, Kill. Everybody know yo' ass be telling us to show up thirty minutes earlier than we supposed to. That's why we always show up thirty minutes later." Boston chuckled, and they slapped hands.

"As long as on time. Now, let's get this meeting started," Kill said and then we all headed inside through the back glass door.

We went to the living room to start up our smoke session and talk about ways for us to wash all of the dirty money that was coming in. A nigga like me didn't see the point in the shit, but Kill was the type of motherfucker that liked to do everything a certain type of way. Since he was the boss the rest of us just fell in line and played our parts and that was fine with me. As long as my pockets stayed blessed I was never stressed.

Tehani

I stood in my floor length mirror and stared at myself. The only thing I was missing was my cherry lipstick. I had on a black bodycon dress that stopped at my thighs and hugged them just right. My ass was poking in the dress and my titties were sitting up perfect. Of course, the little pudge I had in my stomach was on full display since my dress was so fucking tight. I didn't give a shit though, a bitch looked damn good. Especially with the Givenchy pumps that graced my feet. I had paid top dollars for that shit and I loved the way I looked in them.

I had pulled all my thick hair up into a slick bun with only a few baby hairs escaping around the edges. I had full out beat my face and my highlight was popping. All I needed was my lipstick. I walked over to my make-up table and picked up my favorite one. I pulled the top off and then walked back over to my mirror that I had to stand up at. I rubbed the lipstick across my lips and then rubbed my lips together a few times.

"What do you think?" I turned around and asked Cadence after I was done.

She had been sitting on my bed smacking on a bag of potato chips. I smiled at my friend because she still looked just as innocent as she did when we were only kids and she was twenty-four now. I was only a year older than her. If she knew all of the shit I had been involved in growing up she probably wouldn't even be here right now. I know everyone has their problems, but damn. I think the lord skipped a person and gave me an extra load of the fuck shit because I always stayed in something.

This was probably the most lowkey I had been in my life and believe me when I say, I didn't like lowkey. A girl like me was meant to shine. The stars were the limit. At least, that's the bullshit I had believed for a while. Now I was just like fuck it. It was what it was and whatever happened just happened. I'd been happy as shit when I started living that way too because sometimes you just have to say fuck it and do you. We only live once, and we all are going to the grave alone. Period.

"You look stunning, Tee."

"Thanks, Cady. So how long are you visiting for?" I asked as I ran my hand down the front of my dress, making sure it was smoothed out.

"I figured I'd only be down here for this week. I didn't want to be in your way too much," she said, looking down at her hands.

"Girl, now you just making excuses. You won't be in my way. Don't nobody stay in this damn house, but me. My nigga locked up and he has been for the past two years. We've been together for five years now. We first got together when I was twenty and he was twenty-one. I fell for his wild ass too quick. I mean he made me his in like a day type shit. That's why I believe in that instant-love, but shit went left and landed us where we at today. He's serving fifteen years behind them walls for armed robbery. Now it's up to me to run shit around here and keep the money coming in. Ain't nobody else gone pay these bills and ain't nobody else gone put money on Keef's books. That's a proven fact. You being here is a refresher though. That's all I'm really trying to say. Stay here with me for as long as you want. I mean is there something or someone you have to go back to? I didn't think it was because you did just kind of show up. I figured you had just up and left home and wanted to get away. You can be honest with me, Cady. Like I said, I'm already enjoying your company and it's just your first day."

"Thanks, Tee. That really means a lot to me. I really don't have much to rush home to. My child's father and I are uhm… on bad terms right now.

I really just wanted to get away. So I guess I'm busted." She nervously laughed and then tossed another chip in her mouth.

"I knew it had to be something. Look, haven't shit changed when it comes to us. I know we haven't seen each other in years, but you're still like a sister to me. Once best friends always best friends, right?"

"That's right. Thanks for letting me stay for a little bit though, just until I get my head right and then I'll be on the next plane out of here."

"Enough about that, you good, trust me. Now, go get dressed."

"Go get dressed?" she queried.

"Yes, that's what I said. I have to meet my friend Andrea on the strip at eight sharp tonight. It's five minutes after seven now. You still have time to get ready."

"Didn't you say you was going to get drunk with a wild Latina chick? There is no way I am coming out with you and I'm pregnant."

"Yeah, Andrea is my homegirl. She's been in north Miami her whole life. Her mama left one day and never came the fuck back. Now she's taking care of her younger sister Marsha who's only seventeen."

"And how old is Andrea?"

"Andrea is twenty-one, but she's a tough girl just like me. We actually met down at the bar on the strip last year for her twenty first birthday. I know she's four years younger than me, but the girl can party her ass off."

"Does everyone just have it rough around here?"

"Pretty much. Welcome to the fucking trenches because that's basically where we at. They think they can come in here and build these decent looking homes and that'll fix everything, but at the end of the day this is still the fucking hood. We were just lucky enough over this way that they fixed this shit because if you turn down the wrong road you will see houses and apartment buildings that's fucking older than our grandmothers. Do you get what I'm saying?"

"I feel you."

"So, are you coming? I hate to leave you here alone on your first night. You don't have to drink on the strip. There're other things you can do. You can shop, or you can go and get something to eat. You can eat just about anything because they have so many damn restaurants or you can just do some walking, which would do you and the baby some good." I smiled big at her because I could tell by the look on her face that she had changed her mind.

"Fine, let me go and get ready," she huffed.

"Yasssss! I'm going to drink enough for you and me, baby. Don't even trip!" I couldn't hide my excitement if I wanted to. This had turned out to be a damn good day aside from Kill complaining about his crate this morning. I had fixed that problem though and now I was ready to hit the strip with my two favorite girls.

Andrea

"What the fuck have I told you about wearing my god damn heels, Marsha!" I stormed into the living room of my tiny one-bedroom apartment and yelled.

I was sick of her ass always borrowing my shit. She was only seventeen and that was barely even old enough to go out somewhere. I don't know why she felt like she needed to get dolled up and go out in all of my expensive shit. Money didn't come easy around here and if she wanted nice things then she needed to work for it her damn self.

When I wasn't out partying I was down at the diner busting my fucking ass as a waitress. On slow nights I would even go behind the building with some of the older men just to make some extra change. Shit was hard for me and Marsha. Our mother left and never looked back. That seemed to be a trend around this bitch though. I know ten motherfuckers off the top of my head right now that mothers abandoned them. No one gave a fuck these days, not even mothers.

I told my little sister that I could barely afford to take care of us so the last thing she had better come into this apartment with was a damn baby. The day that happened is the day that she was going to be on her own. I told her I had her back and I would make sure she was straight until she hit eighteen, but the little bitch is just reckless. She already thinks she's grown, and I really can't tell her ass shit, so the day she pops out with a baby is the day our deal is off.

"Man, what you talking about? I ain't trying to hear that shit right now," Marsha looked up and said. Basically brushing me off.

Her friend Jayohna was over and they were smoking on a blunt that they were passing back and forth. I didn't give a shit about them smoking because I had much bigger problems to deal with. Hell, I was smoking at the age of fifteen, so I was cool with it. A little weed never hurt nobody. I just hated when the two of them would get together because there was no telling what the fuck they would get into.

Plus, they messed around with these older dudes that they had no fucking business talking to, but I ain't nobody mama so don't nobody listen to my ass. Hell, Jayohna's brother stayed in the streets. I knew for a fact that he had to know that his sister be out in the streets too doing whatever the fuck she wanted to do, and Marsha was the same way.

If Jaydon didn't care about his sister being out here in these streets then neither did I. I couldn't even control my own sister, so I knew I wasn't about to try to control his. If he stayed his ass from in between Tehani's legs maybe he could do something about his sister. Instead, the only thing he was doing was making his girl Madden look like a fool. I guess her name was Madden for a reason because she stayed getting played by a nigga.

"I don't give a fuck what your shit head ass is in the mood to hear. Keep your scarecrow feet out of my expensive heels. You always scuff them up! Now I can't even wear these because I don't have time to scrub them with a toothbrush. Stupid ass Punta!"

"You a Punta!"

"Ya mammy!" I yelled back to her as I walked back down the narrow hall to my bedroom.

When I got in my bedroom I walked over to the wall where I kept my shoes lined up at. I saw a pair of heels that would work with my outfit just as good as the other ones and slid them on. I had on a black half shirt with a short skirt to match. I had straightened my long black hair so that it was lying flat down.

My light tan colored skin shimmered from the make-up I had on, making my brown eyes pop. I was on the slim side, but that didn't mean I ain't have no body. I had a few curves. Marsha looked just like me accept she was a teen version. We both looked just like our no-good ass mama.

"Where you about to ride out to?" Marsha quizzed when I walked back in the living room.

"I'm going to have drinks on the strip with Tehani. Don't wait up for me because I plan to get some dick tonight."

"I hope not from my brother's homeboy Boston," Jayohna said and then pursed her lips. She may have been a kid, but her little ass stayed in the mix, so I was all ears for what she knew.

"Why you say that, Jay?" I asked.

"Because he stay talking mad shit about you being his loyal side hoe. Plus, you know the nigga got a whole fucking family, sis. Why even entertain that nigga? Y'all hoes be real sickening."

"Jay, stay in a child's place, you don't even know the half of what it's like once you're really grown and reality kicks in. Lucky for you, you'll probably never have to find out because of that rich ass trapping brother of yours."

"Whatever. You can't say I ain't try to put your dumb ass up on game. What's wrong with these bitches, Marsha? We younger than them and got more fucking sense. The shit don't make no sense. Y'all just dumb, for real. Out here doing anything to keep a nigga with money," Jayohna ranted.

"Shut the fuck up! Sick of you little bitches." I grabbed my things off the counter and then headed to the front door.

"Ay, you can give me a ride home, Drea?" Jayohna asked and Marsha started laughing.

"After all of the shit you were just talking I should make your ass walk. Come the fuck on before I change my mind. Marsha don't be fucking on my couch while I'm gone!" I warned.

"I'mma fuck in ya bed then because unlike you I'm actually getting some dick tonight," Marsha bragged.

"I'mma beat nasty fucker! Come on, Jay!" The two of them together were going to drive me wild if all the drinking I do didn't. Jesus take the wheel.

Forty minutes later I was pulling into the parking garage. I had dropped Jayohna off at home and then headed straight here. I had a bottle in my lap that I had popped open at a stop sign. It burned so good and I drunk on it all the way until I had got here. I had a nice little buzz going on and I was ready to get more drinks in me. I got out of the car and locked it before running my hands down my hair and adjusting my clothes.

The walk to the strip was a short one. It was right across from the parking garage that charged you forty fucking dollars just to park. The shit was ridiculous, but it was worth it. If you didn't park in the garage you would end up parking miles away. No one wanted to walk miles just to get to the strip when you're were going to walk some more once you got to the strip.

The strip was like a big ass playground for adults. It had ten bars, twenty restaurants, over twenty-five shopping centers and t-shirt stands. There was a Ferris-wheel at the very end of it that lit up the whole strip brighter than it already was. The shit even had bartenders that would walk up and down the strip selling drinks and taking orders. It was a real lit ass scene that stayed packed regularly.

I found Tehani at the very first bar on the strip. She had already ordered us drinks and she was up dancing to the smooth music that was playing. I joined right in with her after taking my drink out of her hand. The party had just started, and I couldn't wait to forget about my shitty ass life that I could only escape through drugs and liquor.

Cadence

When we first got to the strip I was amazed. It was so beautiful, and it reminded me a lot of home. There were people everywhere out enjoying themselves. The weather was perfect, and it just felt good to be out in a city where no one recognized me. I stopped and got myself some cotton candy to smack on while I walked up the strip. I wanted to see everything. It was the first time since the situation back at home that I felt normal again.

Before things took a turn for the worse back home I was working down at the hospital as a radiologic technologist in other words a rad tech. I had taken an early leave from work because truthfully it had just started to get stressful. I don't feel like it was really the job that was stressing me out, but instead it was Lennox. I met Lennox after I had graduated high school. I was eighteen at the time and he was twenty-two.

He was so charming when we first met. He was older and that was a plus for me. He had chocolate skin just a tad bit darker than mine. Add a slight muscular build to that and a long beard and you had Lennox. He was a crime scene investigator and he was very passionate about his work. He talked about it often and he stayed up late every night going over things for work. It didn't bother me though. I was just a young girl in love, smitten with what was right in front of me.

The first year of our relationship was beautiful, but all the years to follow that year were pure hell. Work became less of Lennox's passion and more of his headache. It seemed the only way he could blow off some steam was beating on me or downing me in some type of way. It was like my misery became his pleasure. As time went on things only got worse. I tried my best to work things out with him and deal with his crazy ways that were so new to me, and I did for a while. I did all the way up until things got out of my control and left me with no option but to flee.

An image of blood everywhere popped up in my head and I closed my eyes tight to make the visual go away. No matter what I did the visual just kept popping up in my head at the most unwanted times. If I could I would prevent myself from ever having to see such vile things, but once you saw something like what I had witnessed, you just couldn't forget it.

When I opened my eyes back up the first thing I saw was a familiar face. It was the guy from Tehani's house earlier that morning. Even though I was eager to know more about him I still was upset about the way he had tried to play me. Somehow, his eyes found mine in the crowd and I quickly ducked my head down. I was standing right next to a t-shirt stand so I tried my best to hide behind it.

"You do know your belly is still sticking out, right?" a deep voice asked, and I knew it was him before I even peeped around the t-shirt stand.

"It looks like you caught me." I threw my hands in the air and smiled nervously. Something about him just made my heart want to hop right out of my chest. At least that's what it felt like with how fast my heart was beating.

"The baby gave you away. He likes me already," he joked.

"Sure."

"What you hiding for though? I ain't nobody to hide from, unless you owe me some money."

"Well, I didn't want you coming over here and bothering me," I admitted.

"I'd never do no shit like that. I noticed you were alone, and I came to see if you wanted to hang with me, my homeboy Jaydon and his girl Madden. I'm really feeling like a fucking third wheel and I'm starting to regret letting Jaydon talk me into coming with them. So do me this one solid, and I'll owe you one."

"You'll owe me one? You don't even know me."

"Of course I do, we met this morning. I tried to ask you out on a date, but you weren't used to being asked out, so you started acting funny and shit."

"Did you really just go there again?"

"Kill!" a guy yelled that was standing right across from us.

"Here I come, nigga!" he yelled back and before I knew it I felt him grab my hand and pull me in the direction he had started walking. *Was he serious right now and was all the guys in North Miami this straight forward?*

Killian

"Damn, nigga, why you hollering my name out like that for?" I asked Jaydon as soon as I had made it back over to him and Madden.

"Shit, a nigga hungry. I had to speed up the process with you and your friend," Jaydon said, and his eyes went straight to Cadence's stomach. I already knew what he was thinking when he looked back over to me. I paid him no attention though.

I know I had vowed to stay away from Cadence but once I laid eyes on her on the strip I knew I wasn't going to be able to do that. Everything inside of me was pulling me towards that damn girl. That's why I marched right over to her. My lifestyle was complicated, but I would just have to keep her away from that side of things. The only thing she needed to know about was my businesses, those were legit.

Plus, I just couldn't have everybody knowing how deep I really was in the streets. Outside of the hood I was known as a legit business man and that was it. That was the way I planned to keep it too. Of course, if somehow Cadence decided to give me a chance I would tell her the truth eventually, but that just wasn't necessary right now. Hell, if I'm being honest I wasn't even sure if I was ready to start back dating. My heart was full of hurt, but something about Cadence felt right. If I didn't at least give it a try I would always be stuck wondering what if and I just wasn't no what if type of nigga. I made shit happen.

"Cadence, this is my dumbass homeboy, Jaydon and his girl Madden."

"Hey, nice to meet y'all," Cadence said sweetly like I hadn't basically forced her to join us. I was sick of being the third wheel and she was alone so there was no reason why she couldn't join us. At least that's how I felt. On the bright side, she had yet to pull her hand away from mine. That told me everything I needed to know, there was a chance.

"Nice to meet you too," Jaydon and Madden said in unison and Cadence gave them a shy smile. She definitely wasn't shy. I had witnessed her feisty side up close and personal at Tehani's crib.

"You hungry? You eating on that cotton candy like you think somebody gone take it," I joked. I looked down at her and she scrunched up her forehead.

"Maybe it's just good. No, I'm not hungry." She slid her hand out of mine and that's when I knew she easily got offended. It was just like earlier.

"Have you eaten any real food?" I interrogated. I wasn't going to pay her little slight tantrum any attention.

"No."

"Okay, well we are going to eat. That baby doesn't want no damn cotton candy. He wants some real food. Ain't that right, man?" I don't know what made me do it, but I placed my hand on her stomach and I was met with a gentle kick.

It was like Cadence stopped breathing as we just stared at each other. An intense feeling, that I couldn't describe if I wanted to, shot through my body and just by looking at Cadence I could tell that she had felt it too. Neither of us said anything or pulled away from each other. We just stood there caught up in our moment. I thought about my daughter and sadness washed over me. I slowly pulled my hand away and cleared my throat.

"My bad, I should have uhm, asked before I just touched your stomach. I know some women don't like that shit."

"No, it's okay. My baby likes you. The only problem is you keep calling her a he when she's a she. Whenever she likes someone she will move for them. If not she would have tried to move to the other side away from your hand and I'll be honest, she doesn't move for anyone but me. So it shocked me that she kicked for you."

"She just heard me talking about food. That's all that is," I laughed, trying to shake the sadness off.

I looked at Cadence and her bright eyes warmed my heart just a little. Before I met her a woman was the last thing on my mind. The one I had given my heart to had hurt me the worst, but here Cadence was bringing me a little peace on the inside and she didn't even know it. She made me feel better and she was a complete stranger. That alone made me want to be around her more.

Then, I wouldn't drown in my own sorrows because that's all I had been doing over the last year. I had no idea how I managed to push forward daily, I'd just done it. It seemed like Cadence could give my life purpose again and I needed that more than anything. The darkness was trying to take over me and she was that little light that could possibly pull me out. I wanted to say my feelings were playing tricks with me, but that couldn't be the case. I had come in contact with numerous women, even some pregnant ones, and none of them had made me feel like this.

"Y'all ready to go get something to eat now or y'all just gone stand there smiling at each other?" Jaydon questioned.

"Yeah, we can go get something to eat," Cadence spoke up. She smiled at me and I knew she was no longer upset about my cotton candy joke.

Jaydon and Madden walked in front of us while we followed behind them with a small gap in between us. I took that time to talk to Cadence a little bit. We were walking down the strip trying to figure out which restaurant we wanted to eat at. Well, more like Jaydon and Madden was arguing about which restaurants not to eat at. I knew that I wouldn't be going nowhere else with the two of them for a while. They just couldn't get their shit together and there was nothing worse than being around a couple that constantly argued about the dumbest shit. It was nerve wrecking.

"So, I just want to apologize about earlier at Tehani's house. I don't know if I offended you or what, but it was nothing like that. It's just that you seemed so shocked that I would ask a pregnant chick out. I mean you ain't have no ring on your finger so in my eyes you were available."

"I'll admit that I was a little offended by your snide remark. It sounded like you were trying to play me."

"Nah, never that."

"Yeah, okay. I'm just not used to being asked out by anyone. Hell, men see I'm pregnant and look the other way so fast." She laughed, and the shit was contagious. I couldn't help but laugh with her.

"I've witnessed that before."

"Exactly."

"But what I'm hearing is that you are single for a fact?"

"I'm definitely all alone," she mumbled so low that I barely heard her.

I decided not to say anything back. Instead I grabbed her hand again and she let me. I was damn near thirty feeling like a young nigga back in high school when he wanted a girl. I ain't give a fuck though because I always got what I wanted and wasn't shit about to be different with Cadence. It just came with the territory of being a boss. I ain't give a fuck about her being pregnant. I was going to make her mine. After everything I had gone through I was down for taking it slow and I was going to make sure she knew that.

"So how old are you?" I asked, finally making conversation again.

"I'm twenty-four. What about you?"

"I'm twenty-nine."

"Cool."

"What did you do back home?"

"Huh?" She stopped walking mid stride and her eyes got big as fifty cent pieces.

"What was your occupation?"

"Oh." She nervously laughed and then visually relaxed.

Something was definitely fishy about her background; I just couldn't put my finger on it. She seemed like a genuine person, but something had happened. If I could get her to open up to me I knew for a fact that I would be able to help her. She was scared of something; I just didn't know what. All I did know is that if she was scared of something, she had to be running from something or someone. That just didn't sit right with me. I was so used to always being able to handle shit on my time, and if something was getting handled on my time, it was getting handled ASAP.

I wanted to save her, but how could I when I didn't know what I was saving her from? Why did I want to save this girl so badly? Most importantly why did I feel like she was the one that was going to save me? I had only known Cadence for one day, yet all of these things were running through my head.

"I'm sorry, what was we talking about?" I asked, completely thrown off track by my thoughts that quick.

"I'm a rad tech. I used to work at the hospital back at home. What about you?"

"I'm a business man," I replied.

"Y'all cool with eating here?" Madden turned around and asked as we walked up on this restaurant.

"Shit, are y'all cool with eating here is the real question?"

"You got jokes, Kill." Jaydon laughed.

"I'm just saying. A nigga sick of y'all shit. Don't invite me to come nowhere else with y'all ass."

Everybody laughed as we walked into the restaurant. We got a table for four right away and I ordered myself a shot off the top shelf. Cadence ordered a water and a virgin strawberry daiquiri. The warm look she had in her eyes before had returned. I smiled at her and she smiled back.

"I can't believe what I'm seeing. Kill are you actually smiling at somebody because I swear we don't get shit but a mug. Us and everybody else around you. You must be really special, girl," Madden said, after ordering her drink.

"Mind yo' business nosey ass girl," Jaydon fussed, and Madden rolled her eyes.

"What? I'm just saying it's good to see somebody be able to make him smile. You know after everything."

"I appreciate it, Madden," I quickly said.

She looked at me and mouthed a sorry before giving her menu all of her attention. Jaydon shook his head and I gave him a little nod to let him know shit was straight. She didn't mean no harm and I felt what she was saying. It had been a while since anybody had made me truly smile from the heart. A mug was my permanent expression most of the time. I didn't do it on purpose I just didn't have shit to smile about and it had been that way since the death of my daughter.

"This looks good," Cadence said, pointing at something on the menu.

"Why don't you try it out?" I asked her.

"Oh I plan to," she smiled.

A couple of hours passed by before we were done eating and talking to each other. The vibe was chill, and I had a way better night than I had expected when I first agreed to come out with Jaydon and Madden. If I hadn't I wouldn't have run into Cadence, and she was the best part about the night. We had just walked out the restaurant when I saw trouble walking over to us in a pair of fucking heels.

"Cadence!" Tehani hollered out loud, sipping on a drink almost as big as her damn head.

Tehani

Andrea and I had spent a couple of hours on the strip hitting up all the bars that we could. We were pretty lit, and my head was starting to spin a little bit. That's when I knew it was time to go. Plus, I hadn't seen Cadence anywhere on the strip and I had called her phone about five times. She had about three voicemails from me. I had no idea what I had said on them because the liquor was basically talking for me. I didn't want to seem like a party pooper, but I needed to find her. My nerves were shot, and I was over drinking.

"Are you okay?" Andrea questioned as she leaned her head down on my shoulder, I was practically holding her ass up.

Somehow, she had managed to get way drunker than me. I didn't see how that was possible when we had drunk the same amount. Then again, knowing Andrea her ass had probably started drinking before she got here. Liquor and drugs were her way of escaping the life that she was living. That wasn't the case with me, drinking was my way of having a little fun and nothing more.

"No, I need to find Cadence." We were walking back down the strip and I had yet to spot her. "I knew I should have just stayed with her. I didn't want her to be around all the drinking we were going to be doing though. She's not like that at all."

"Well, I haven't met her yet, but I can tell by the pictures you showed me that she's a good girl. I remember when I used to be a good girl." Andrea was slurring her words as she talked, but I allowed her to just ramble on. As long as she continued to walk we were good. "Never mind, I take that back."

"You take what back?" I looked down at her like she was crazy.

"I was never a good girl. I tried to actually remember a time when I was, and I can't remember shit. I've always been young and reckless, and the way things are going for me ain't shit changing, but my age." She laughed.

"You can change too. You just have to really want it."

"Okay, Tee, don't start with one of your drunk lectures. I ain't changing and shit you ain't either."

"Bitch, I never said I was trying to change. I'm good just the way I am."

"I can agree with that. Hey, is that her right there!" Andrea suddenly perked up and started pointing in the direction of one the most expensive restaurants on the strip. I squinted my eyes and it was definitely Cadence… along with some friends. I smirked so hard my jaws ached.

"Cadence!" I hollered once we were a little closer. I took a sip of the big ass drink I had been trying to finish while looking for her. It was hard to drink it when I had to hold Andrea ass up and since my head was starting to spin I really didn't want it anymore anyway. "Here, you want the rest of this?" I offered my drink to Andrea which probably wasn't the best idea since she was already fucked up.

"You know I do, Mami." She eagerly grabbed the drink out of my hands as we neared Cadence.

"Cady, I have been looking all over for you. I've called your phone like five times! You had me worried something had happened!"

She pulled her phone out and looked at it before saying, "I'm sorry, Tehani. I haven't looked at my phone since I ran into Kill. I figured you would be having so much fun that you wouldn't even remember I came here with you." She lightly chuckled.

"Well, you're wrong. You're down here in Florida with me and ain't shit gone happen to you on my watch. It's literally gone have to be over my dead body. I know I party hard, but all the liquor in the world couldn't make me forget about you. I know we just now linking back up, but you're family and I'll protect you with my life." I gently grabbed her and wrapped my arms around her.

If anything had happened to her I was going to flip. I couldn't even blame the liquor because I was always protective over the ones I cared about. When I couldn't find her I had automatically started assuming the worst, but now that I knew she was okay it was time to have some fun.

"Thanks, Tee. It's really good to know that you still have my back just like when we were younger," Cadence expressed.

"Once I'm riding for you I'mma always ride for you. You know that."

"You're right." She agreed.

"Hey Jaydon," I said softly, my smirk reappearing.

His girlfriend was pretty but pretty didn't stop a motherfucker from being dumb. I knew Madden and we had even gone to school together. We were just never cool. She was the uppity chick who thought she was better than everybody else and I was the ratchet one who was with all the dumb shit. Our worlds were completely different and the only thing we had in common now was her nigga. Jaydon gave me a little head nod and Madden's eyes almost popped out of her head.

"What the fuck is going on here?" she quizzed, staring dead at Jaydon.

"Not shit, just speaking to a friend. Girl, you need to relax." I smiled.

"You don't tell me what the fuck I need to do. It's other people standing here and the first person you choose to speak to is Jay?"

"Well, I don't fuck with you. I never have, and I never will. So tell me why the fuck I would speak to you? What's up, Kill?"

"Tehani, gone head with that extra shit, damn. Messy as a motherfucker, shit don't make no sense at your age." Kill huffed. I don't even know why I had bothered speaking to his ass. Rude was that nigga's middle name.

"Damn, since when did speaking to somebody become a crime? Cadence, you ready because I'm about to go?" Kill had sucked all the fun out of me fucking with Jaydon and his girlfriend. Hell, we all knew I was being messy, but he ain't have to call me the fuck out. That's why I ain't like his ass now. He always thought he had to speak on some shit with his dumbass.

"Yeah, I'm ready," Cadence said to me before turning to face Kill. "Thanks for a fun night. I guess you're not that bad after all," she joked, smiling big as hell.

"Shitting me." I mumbled, and Andrea laughed.

"You'll have to give me a chance to do it again sometime, beautiful. What's your number?" Kill asked Cadence, but I interjected before she could answer.

"None of business. If you want her you gone have to work a little harder than that. Yo pockets long and you different from these other niggas, remember? Well, come at her better!" I grabbed Cadence's hand and pulled her away.

I had no idea what Kill's plans was when it came to Cadence, but I knew for a fact he would have to find another way to get at her if he really wanted her. Cadence was just too willing which was probably how she ended up pregnant and beefing with her baby daddy or whatever the hell they had going on. You had to make these niggas work for shit out here or else they would do the bare minimum when it came to you. That wasn't going to be the case when it came to my best friend because I wasn't having it.

"Tell Boston and his family Andrea says hi," Andrea said to Kill and Jaydon before following behind us.

"Wait, what if I actually wanted to give him my number?" Cadence asked.

"You can't give it to him that easy, Cady. Make him work for it and see what he's really about first. If he's really into you this little mess that happened tonight won't stop a thing. Trust me, have I ever steered you wrong?" I quizzed.

"Actually, you have," she said, making me laugh.

"Yeah, well that was forever ago. I ain't know shit then, but I know a lot more now. Lucky for you I'm willing to share my knowledge on these niggas."

"She might actually want to give the nigga a chance, Tee. All you do is play with these niggas," Andrea butted in.

"Mind yo' business, Drea!" I turned around and yelled to her. "You fuck with married niggas, so yo' input don't matter in this situation."

"Why do I feel like I'm with the 'City Girls' or some shit? *I'll take your man, don't play with me hoe!*" Cadence mocked the 'City Girls' from a famous hip-hop duo that was popping. Andrea and I both hysterically started laughing at her as we made our way to the parking garage finally. "I'm serious," she said, cracking us up even more.

Cadence had a lot to learn, but she would be alright with me by her side. I didn't know what the problem with her child's father was, but I knew it had to be bad and I knew things had to be over with them. She had been here for a whole day and I hadn't even seen her on the phone with the nigga once. Plus, she seemed pretty interested in Kill and not interested and fixing whatever her problem was and that spoke for itself.

Lennox

It had been two whole weeks since my baby mama disappeared in the night. The bitch was five months pregnant with my baby and had the audacity to run the fuck off. I didn't know where the fuck she was at or what the hell she thought she was doing, but when I found the bitch I was going to drag her ass back home by the hair. She'd be lucky if I didn't kill her after the stunt she had pulled. She'd never tried anything like this, and I was going to make sure it was her last time trying it.

Normally, Cadence wouldn't even breathe without me telling her that she could do so. I whooped her ass daily to make sure she never defied me. I'm the type of man who has to have control over my woman. If I can't, then you probably not the woman for me. Don't get me wrong I'm a loyal ass nigga. I just can't keep myself from beating the living shit out of my woman when she makes me mad.

Cadence knew I loved her though and one of us was going to have to be six-feet under before this shit ended with us. We had been together for six years and that's time I could never get back. It's not like I wanted that time back anyway, I just wanted my bitch back home with me and I wouldn't stop until that happened. Even thinking about her pulling this shit pissed me the fuck off.

Boom! Boom! Boom!

"I'm coming!" I heard Cadence's mother yell out.

"Hey, I'm sorry to keep coming over here unannounced like this," I said as soon as she opened the door for me.

"Hey, Lennox, you still haven't heard anything from Cady yet?"

"No ma'am, have you?"

"Not since she stopped by that night acting weird and telling me not to worry about her. She said she was leaving for a bit and she would be in touch."

"She told you she was leaving that night she stopped by? Why the fuck is you just now saying something about this shit!"

"Excuse me?" Mrs. Montgomery was looking at me like she wanted to lay me over her leg and whoop me. I had to quickly regain my composure before I spoke again.

"I'm sorry, Mrs. Montgomery. I didn't mean to talk to you that way—"

"I know you didn't." She interrupted. A stern look was on her face as she pulled her robe closed tighter than it already was. She pushed her glasses up on her nose and stared at me.

"I didn't. I'm just frustrated and now all of a sudden you're telling me that she told you that she was leaving. I've been over here every day for two weeks straight and not once did you mention she said she was leaving."

"I understand your frustration, but I will not be disrespected. Especially not in my own home. Now, Lennox, you're alright with me and you take good care of my daughter, but don't you ever use that tone with me again. Do you understand me?"

"Yeah, I understand. I truly am sorry."

I tried to turn on the charm that I usually used with Cadence's mother, but I could tell that she was looking at me a little different now. She was always so soft spoken and proper when I came over, so I didn't see the change up coming. I guess she was like any other parent and didn't put up with no mess. I could respect that, but my focus was on her dumbass daughter.

"I don't know what the two of you have going on or what y'all was going through before she left, but she looked tired. Maybe, she just needed a vacation. I know for a fact she would have told me if anything was wrong, so I don't think you have anything to worry about."

"How can I be sure of that? I tried to file a missing person report, but after they talked to me and came over and saw that she had taken her things and left in the car they summed it up to me getting left in the wind. After that I couldn't get shit done about her going missing. I know they called and talked to you and I guess you just helped them decide that she had left me."

"I told them that she told me she was leaving for a little bit and for me not to worry. I know my child and every once in a blue moon she likes to do something spontaneous. I figured this is what this is."

I could feel myself getting angry. I had been over to this woman's house so many times. Every time I came she told me the same bullshit. She hadn't talked to Cadence, but she would let me know if she did. In my head, I felt like that meant she didn't know any more than I did. The whole time she knew a hell of a lot more than me. It was pissing me off because I had wasted two whole weeks trying to convince the cops that Cadence hadn't just up and left me.

If I had known what I know now I would have taken a completely different approach with things. I knew Mrs. Montgomery was getting old and she was forgetful, but she hadn't forgot to mention that her daughter told her she was leaving to the cops. So why in the fuck would she forget to mention it to me? I wanted to snatch her up and choke her until she took her last breath, but if I'd done that I would have to do the same to Cadence's father... and he was too fucking big for that. Therefore, the best thing for me to do was leave and get myself together.

"Well, thanks for your time, Mrs. Montgomery. I'm going to get on home now. All of this is just a lot to deal with. The love of my life is gone, and she has my baby in her stomach. Now I know nothing happened to her and she just left. She didn't leave a note or anything, she just left me to worry. I don't know what I'm going to do without her." I fake got choked up while I was saying the last part, but inside I was really boiling hot.

"It's going to be okay, Lennox. She'll be back, just give her this time alone. Pregnancy can take a toll on people sometimes, maybe she just needed her space for a couple of weeks. Y'all weren't having problems at home were you?"

"No, everything was great... or so I thought."

"Well, there you go. You say y'all weren't having problems and she didn't mention anything about y'all having problems to me. You clearly don't have anything to worry about."

"How don't I have anything to worry about when she hasn't even called me?"

"She hasn't called me either. That's why I figure she needed a little time alone. I've never been one to pry into Cadence's life. She's grown now, so I let her do her own thing and trust that she will come to me if she's having a problem. I know this may be hard for you because y'all are together and you haven't heard from her, but just give her this time. She'll come back home. I'll let you know if I hear anything from her."

"I guess you're right, but okay have a good night."

"You do the same, baby." She closed the door and it took everything in me not to kick that bitch right the fuck down.

I headed back to my car even angrier than before. Cadence was going to make me kill her ass and that's exactly what I had set in my head to do as soon as I got my hands on her. I ain't know where the fuck she was at but once I found her it was going to be hell to pay. No one walked out on me and to make things worse my brother had been missing for two weeks as well. Something wasn't right, but I do know one thing, the both of them had better not be together or I was going to be investigating both of their fucking crime scenes.

Cadence

I walked into the kitchen to get myself a bottled water. When I did the smell of pineapples hit my nose and I had to rush to the bathroom. I puked my guts out for a few minutes before getting myself together and returning to the kitchen. When I did I saw Tehani posted up by the stove looking right at me. I gave her a small smile as I walked over to the fridge and grabbed myself a bottle of water. Then, I went to the kitchen table and took a seat.

"Are you okay?" Tehani inquired.

"Yes, I'm fine."

"Well, why did you go throw up after walking in here? I heard you in the bathroom."

"Truthfully, it was the smell of those damn pineapples." I giggled.

"Oh, uh uh. What you got against my pineapples? You know that has been my favorite fruit since I was like five."

"I know that, but you have been adding pineapples to dinner every night for two weeks straight. My baby is sick of pineapples and now she's making me sick after even smelling them."

"See that's where you're wrong. We weren't even eating pineapples tonight. I was going to put our food in a pineapple bowl. Don't do me."

She turned around and started stirring whatever she was cooking on the stove.

I grabbed a paper towel that was laying on the table in front of me and crumbled it up before tossing it at her head. Since she was across the kitchen the paper towel ball didn't make it anywhere near her. She had turned around to say something as soon as the paper towel ball hit the floor. She looked at me with a shocked expression before she busted out laughing.

"I guess I'm caught," I said.

"Cadence you so fucking stupid. I've been laughing none stop these last couple of weeks. I'm really glad you're still here."

"Thanks, Tee."

"No problem, but I do want to ask you something." I could tell by the look in her eyes that she was about to start questioning me.

For some reason she had become real concerned about what was going on back home before I came to visit. Every time she got ready to ask me something I had to make up an excuse and dismiss myself. It may have been two weeks since everything happened, and I found myself here, but I still wasn't ready to open up about what had really transpired the night I ran away from my home state. Lucky for me my phone started ringing and I answered it as fast as I could.

"Hello?"

"What's up, Cady?" Kill asked, making me smile just from the sound of his voice.

He had popped up at Tehani's house the very next day after the night on the strip. Tehani was shocked and I was too a little bit. I just knew after I had allowed Tehani to pull me away from him that he wouldn't want to talk to me. Turns out Tehani was right, if a man really wants you he will work to get you. Kill had stopped by everyday just to sit on Tehani's porch swing with me and talk.

He always brought me ice cream or something sweet when he came because he knew I had a bad sweet tooth. He would bring it and then fuss if I ate too much of it. I swear he could be my personal doctor because he stayed telling me what was good for the baby and what wasn't. I had yet to see the other side of him that Tehani felt the need to warn me about. When he was with me and it was just us he was more relaxed, but once someone else would come in our presence he would harden right back up and become very alert. That told me that he may have had some slight trust issues.

He still hadn't mentioned what happened with his daughter to me yet and I made sure not to bring it up. I wanted to so badly, but I knew it wasn't my place to do so. I had to just let him open up about it to me first. He still carried that hurt look in his eyes, but when we were together it was like he would come back to life right in front of my eyes. The hurt look would still be there, but it would be accompanied by a hopeful look. I was sure I brought him hope that things would be okay.

What he didn't know was that just like I brought him hope he brought me a feeling of security. It was like whenever I was with him my past didn't matter and it didn't eat away at my mind like it did when he wasn't around. I wasn't fearful that my past would catch me because with him I would be living in the present and that would be the only thing that mattered at the time. Even when I was with Lennox I had never felt so secure before. It was a refreshing and nice feeling.

"Not much, about to eat. What are you up to?" I asked sweetly.

"On the way to handle a little business right now, but I was thinking after I was done, and you were finished eating I could stop by and pick you up and we could chill at my crib for a little bit," he suggested.

"I would love that, just let me know when you on the way."

"Bet, I'll see you soon." He hung up the phone and I pulled my cell away from my ear and placed it on the table.

"What is your boyfriend bringing you for dessert today?" Tehani questioned, grinning at me.

"He is not my boyfriend and he's not bringing me anything. He's going to take me over to his place, so we can chill or whatever."

"Kill say he trying to get some of that pregnant pussy, baby. I ain't mad at him!"

"Shut up, no he not." I laughed.

"You know I have to mess with you. Kill not my favorite person, but I like y'all together."

"We are not together for the millionth time."

"Shit y'all might as well be. Y'all have been spending every single day together since you got here. I knew you was into him that very first day."

"Not this again! I really wasn't into him then; he had just piqued my interest that's all. Once we ran into each other on the strip things changed and for some reason things felt right with him."

"Girl, do you hear yourself? How are things going to feel right with a stranger?"

"I really don't know, Tee, but what I do know is I felt something between us. It was like a spark. You would have to experience it for yourself to know exactly what I'm talking about."

"I guess you're right. I like y'all together though. Cady Cay and Killy Kill."

"Oh my god, you are so corny for that and I thought I was the corny one."

"You is, that bullshit just rubbing off on me!"

"Whatever."

"So, have you talked to your child's father or anyone back home?" she hurriedly asked.

"Welp, I have to go get in the shower. I'll be back down to eat before Kill comes to get me."

I quickly stood up and scurried out of the kitchen before Tehani could say anything else. I knew she was still standing in the same spot shaking her head once I walked out. I didn't care though. I was willing to do anything to avoid having that conversation as long as I could. If Tehani found out what I had done back home she would probably kick me right out of her house and being homeless was the last thing I needed. I walked to my bedroom and gathered my things up for my shower.

Once I was in the shower and the hot water was falling down on me I began to cry. The tears just came back to back and wouldn't stop. As soon as I closed my eyes the image of blood everywhere reappeared in my head. I didn't even realize I had started screaming until I heard Tehani banging at the door asking if I was okay. I opened my eyes back up, heavily heaving as I tried to catch my breath to answer her.

"Cady, you got one second to say something before I kick this damn door down!" Tehani yelled out.

"I'm fine," I croaked.

I swallowed a few times and then hollered out that I was fine again and that I thought I had saw a bug. When I didn't hear her at the door anymore I sighed loudly. I was going to have to get myself together. This much stress couldn't be good for my baby. I hated the situation I was in, but I was going to make the best of it for as long as I could.

Killian

Twenty minutes after I had gotten off the phone with Cadence I pulled up to the back of one of my restaurants. I parked and hopped out of the car. I went to the back exit of the restaurant and put in the code to open the door. When I got inside I went straight to my office that was located in the back. I closed the door behind me and then slid my shirt over my head. I neatly laid it on the couch that was in my office.

I walked over to the closet and pulled out a black t-shirt and a black pair of joggers. I finished getting undressed before putting on the clothes I had pulled out the closet. I walked over to another closet and grabbed a pair of white and black J's out. After I was done putting my shoes on at my desk I pulled out the bottom drawer and grabbed my gun. I stood up and stretched and then placed the gun on my side.

I walked around my desk and headed out of my office. I cracked my neck a couple of times as I walked into the kitchen. When everyone saw me walking in they quickly tried to start working. I appreciated my staff, but what I didn't appreciate was motherfuckers doing shit behind my back. I didn't even crack the slightest smile as I walked over to the cook's station.

When I walked up he wasn't even cooking shit. He was posted up on the counter talking on his phone like he was at home or some shit. I mean this nigga had his shit on speakerphone and all. I didn't even say shit. I just stood off to the side and looked at him. He was already on my shit list as it was, and this shit right here didn't help in the least bit. I literally stood there for two minutes before the nigga even noticed me.

"Boss man, what's happening?" he asked, smiling big as fuck. All I saw was his fake ass gold grill in his mouth. As much money as I was paying him you would have thought that he would have at least bought a real one.

"Shit, that's what I'm trying to figure out." I cracked my knuckles and glared at him.

"I'mma call you back," he said to the person on the other end of his phone call. He ended the call and then slipped his phone in his back pocket after sliding off the counter top. "That was nothing. We had a little down time, so I was just chilling on the phone for a little bit. I was just about to get back to work." He walked over to the dishwasher and pulled a pan out.

"That won't be necessary," I informed him.

"What you mean?" He placed the pan on the counter and then scratched the top of his head. This mother fucker was really trying to act clueless.

"So you really gone play stupid?"

"Nah, I told you that we had a little down time. That's the only reason I was posted up on the counter like that. I'm a hard worker, Kill. You know that for yourself."

"Gordon, come talk to me in my office." I turned my back on him and walked straight out of the kitchen.

When I was back in my office I took a seat at my desk and then pulled my cellphone out. I sent out a few texts and checked a few emails before I heard a loud knock on my door. I called out for Gordon to come in because I was sure that was who it was. When he walked in I saw fear all in his eyes. Not only did he look scared, but he looked fucking guilty and I knew exactly what he was guilty of.

"Talk to me, boss man. What's going on?" He didn't look at me as he spoke he just stared down at the floor with his hands shoved in his pockets.

"A few months ago I found out that you were selling drugs out of my restaurant like it was some kind of trap house or something. Not only was you slinging dope out my kitchen doors, but you were slinging some weak ass product that didn't even come from me. That was two strikes from the get."

"Ay, I can explain."

"Oh, now you know what the fuck I'm talking about? It ain't no need to explain shit because I don't want to hear shit. I let that shit slide and you know for yourself that I don't let a damn thing slide. The only reason I let it slide then is because of Destiny."

Destiny was my homeboy Boston's wife; Gordon was her first cousin. When he first came home from prison he couldn't find a job. Boston had asked me to hire him as a favor and I did. Gordon was an excellent worker but over time he got way too comfortable and started to do what he wanted and that's how he had ended up in the situation that he was currently in. I had spared him once, but I didn't plan on doing it again. If I gave you a warning you had better let that be the only one because after my first warning came death and I rarely gave warnings to start with.

"So you saying I'm fired? Man, I wasn't even slinging dope out the kitchen like that this time. I would just have a few customers drop by from time to time if I knew I was gone be at work all day." I could tell he was bullshitting me just by listening to him.

"That's exactly what I'm saying. I don't give a fuck about how you did it or why you did it. The point is you did the shit after I had already put a stop to it once. That's basically like you saying fuck me."

"Man, I would never say fuck you! If it wasn't for you I wouldn't have been able to get back on my feet after prison. Ain't nobody else gone hire me. You can't do this to me, just give me one more chance that's all I'm asking," he pleaded.

"You can leave now, leave your apron and hat in the kitchen."

"I got a family to take care of, man!"

"Use that dope you was slinging out my kitchen to do it. Have a good day, Gordon."

He looked like he wanted to say something else, but I'm sure the expression on my face told him to get the hell out of my presence. He hung his head low and walked out of my office. I had no pity for him because this wasn't the first time this shit had happened. I logged into my laptop that sat on my desk and continued with checking my emails. About fifteen minutes had passed by when I heard a light tap at my door. I hollered for whoever it was to come in.

"Hey, Kill, are you busy?" Ambrysha walked in and questioned.

"Nah, what's up?" I closed my laptop and gave her my full attention.

Ambrysha was a pretty, petite, girl. She was the color of hot chocolate and she had the brightest smile. She was a smart girl that worked hard. She went above and beyond as the restaurant manager. She was twenty-three and she knew exactly what her plans in life were. She worked hard to achieve her goals daily. Even when life hit her with the worst of times she still managed to push through with a smile. She was like a little sister to me and I always made sure I looked out for her. She was a good person and those were the people that you wanted to keep close.

"Let me sit down before I tell you this." Ambrysha looked behind her and then closed my office door before walking in front of my desk and taking a seat in the plush chair that sat in the front in of it.

"What's up, you straight?"

"Yes, I'm fine. Did Gordon just get fired? I saw him storming out of here not too long ago pissed off. He decided to give everybody a piece of his mind before he left too. According to him I'm a stuck up bitch that needs to remember that she was born as a crack baby. When we had one of our staff meetings we decided to go out for drinks after. Once we were all drunk we started telling each other about ourselves and sharing private things that we had gone through. Well, that was one of the things I shared with him and I can't believe he would throw it back in my face like that." Ambrysha looked hurt and pissed off.

I felt bad for her because that was something she had told me when I first hired her as the manager. When I interviewed people I liked to get to know them on a more personal level before hiring them and that's the topic our interview had ended up at. As a businessman I felt like I had to hold up a certain image and it was the same in the streets. The only difference was I felt more comfortable in the streets than I ever did when I was handling business and that was a shame. The streets had made me the boss that I was and that was something I could never forget.

"How long ago was it when he left?" I asked, clenching my jaw.

"About ten minutes ago. I heard him mumbling about going home and getting drunk. That's not all though."

"What else happened?"

"Money has been popping up missing for the last few months," she confessed.

"Hold up, hold up, hold up, you say what now?" I leaned forward in my chair because I just knew that I hadn't heard her correctly.

"I know I should have been told you this, but you were going through so much when it first started happening. I didn't want to trouble you with it, and I thought I could catch whoever was stealing the money and make them put it all back. I thought I could fix it, but it only got worse."

"Wait a minute. Exactly when did my money start disappearing because it went from happening a few months ago to you saying something about when the money first started disappearing. Now when you say that you make me feel like it's been more than a few months and what exactly are you getting at? Just spit it all out because you know I don't do no beating around the bush."

"Gordon started stealing money from you a few days after that heartbreaking situation happened. There were weeks at a time where you wouldn't even show up. We all understood that, I mean you visit this restaurant more than you do any of your businesses. We knew you needed a break after that traumatic situation. It wasn't until recently that I finally figured out it was him and the amount of money that is popping up missing has gotten larger and larger. I'm just glad you fired him."

"Ambrysha, why the fuck is you just now coming at me with this shit man? Fuck!" I jumped up out of my seat and headed towards the door. "I won't be back today," I turned around and said before walking out the office door.

I jogged out the back exit and straight to my car. I hopped in and started it up right away. Once I had backed my car into the road I took off toward Gordon's house. I didn't even have to hear how much money he had taken. I knew it was a lot just by looking at Ambrysha. I hated that she hadn't told me sooner, but Ambrysha hated drama and conflict. She knew if she told me I was going to act exactly the way I was now. I didn't play about my fucking money and everybody knew that much.

I pulled up to Gordon's house out in the woods about thirty minutes later. He didn't have any neighbors and he wouldn't even get the chance to wish that he did. I parked my car and got out. I walked to the front door slowly. His car was out front, so I knew he had to be inside. I quickly picked the lock and walked straight into his home. I didn't give a fuck about anyone else being home either. If they were there and they saw my face they were going to die and there was no debating that. Ever since my daughter had been killed I had only become more heartless and that's why it was crazy that I had been letting Cadence in to my personal world.

I eased down the hallway until I spotted Gordon in his kitchen grabbing beer out of the refrigerator. I eased up on him quickly and placed my gun to the back of his head. This nigga had to die. I didn't even say shit or explain myself. He dropped the beer and that told me that he knew it was me that had come for him. I pulled the trigger and then dipped back to my car.

* * *

It was about an hour and a half before I pulled up in front of Tehani's house. I couldn't go and pick Cadence up with blood all over me, so I had to make a stop at the crib first. Once I had showered and changed my clothes I went out to my backyard and burned the clothes I had been wearing. I dropped the dirty gun off in the hood to one of my little homies, so he could get rid of that shit for me. I paid him to do just that. He would always get rid of all of the dirty guns that my crew and I made dirty. Usually he would sell them out of state or just make sure they never popped up again and that's all I needed for him to do. Wes was a young cat that stayed in the streets and his loyalty was never ending.

I got out of my vehicle and went to knock on Tehani's front door. She came to the door quickly and yanked it open. She looked me up and down and then looked back over her shoulder before easing the door open.

"What's good?" I quizzed, looking at her suspiciously.

"Look, I need a favor," she whispered.

"What?"

"Cadence is hiding something, and I don't know what."

"How you figure that?" I asked, even though I had suspected the same thing.

"She just is. Every time I try to ask her about back home she changes the subject, or she walks out of the room."

"Maybe, she just don't want to talk about the shit with you."

"That may be the case. That's why I need you to find out. I'm just a little concerned about her."

"I'm concerned about her too, but the best thing for us to do is chill and let her open up about it. If you force her to give up information she may run from you next."

"Aha, so you think she's running from someone too?"

"I never said that shit."

"Oh, but you did. I think something happened with her and her baby daddy. That has to be who she is running from. Don't tell her I told you this, but she has been waking me up out my sleep every night, sometimes three times a night. She'll just wake up screaming at the top of her lungs and she's always hollering something about Lennox. If you didn't know, Lennox is her baby daddy's name. She did tell me that much."

"All done!" Cadence popped up behind Tehani suddenly and announced. Tehani slightly jumped and I just shook my head.

"How was it?" Tehani asked Cadence and I figured she had just finished eating before she came to the door.

"It was great. You ready, Kill?" Cadence looked at me and asked.

"Yeah, let's ride." Tehani stepped to the side after giving me a look, basically telling me to find out more. I grabbed Cadence's hand as soon as she was out on the porch and led her to my car. I couldn't wait to get back to my spot, so we could chill and vibe.

When I was around Cadence she had a way of making me feel like I could talk to her about anything. She would just look at me with those sweet eyes of hers and smile at me with the kindest smile. I could tell she was a good girl, but just like Tehani had said, something was up with her. Hopefully, I would be able to find out. I wouldn't be able to save her until she told me her real story.

Cadence

When we pulled up to Kill's house I was surprised at how big it was. It was nice, and the inside was even more mind blowing than the outside. If I didn't know it before I definitely knew now that he was a certified boss. Tehani had told me that, but I thought she was over exaggerating, but she definitely wasn't. This man was paid out the ass. None of that mattered to me I just wondered exactly how many businesses did he own?

"Can I get you something to drink?" Kill asked as we sat on the loveseat in his living room.

"Sure, what do you have?"

"I have a little of everything."

"Oh, well water will be fine."

"I knew was gone say that. I don't even know why you asked what I had to drink." He chuckled.

"I don't know, out of curiosity I guess." I smiled at him as he got up to grab me a bottle of water. He came back a few moments later and handed it to me. I took a sip of the water and he sat back down beside me. He pulled my feet in his lap and I immediately pulled them away from him.

"I can't rub your feet for you?"

The way he was looking at me made me want to tell him that he could rub whatever he wanted to on me. I blamed my damn hormones. They were making me so horny and I had never been the type to always want sex, but lately that seemed to be the only thing I wanted. Being around Kill daily wasn't helping either. He was just so damn fine, and his personality only made me want him more, but I managed to control myself.

"Yes, you can." I sat my bottle of water down on the floor beside me and then placed my feet back into his lap.

He pulled my shoes and socks off before he started to give me a foot massage. I laid my head back and enjoyed the pressure that he was applying to my feet. His phone started ringing and he stopped to look at it before putting the phone right back down. I immediately sat up and gave him a suspicious look. I knew he wasn't my boyfriend or anything, but there was no reason for him to hide anything from me.

"What's up?" he asked me, casually.

"Why didn't you answer your phone?" I tried my best not to sound like a jealous girlfriend, but I knew for a fact that I did.

"Shit, that ain't nobody."

"Why are you looking like that then?" I pulled my feet back out of his lap and glared at him.

"Looking like what?"

"I don't know. I've never seen that expression on your face before, but it's something. Kill, you know you can tell me."

"Alright, I'll tell you, but promise me something?"

"Yes, I promise," I said before I knew it.

"You don't even know what I'm about to say."

"My bad." I blushed.

"Promise me you want start showing me any sympathy." I knew right then that he was about to tell me about his daughter. I took a deep breath and tried to prepare myself for what he was going to say.

"I promise," I reiterated.

"That was Tyra calling me."

"Who is Tyra?"

"That's my baby mama."

"Oh."

"Yeah, she keeps calling me from jail and it pisses me off every time she does."

"From jail?"

"Yeah, she killed our two-year-old daughter. Now, she keeps calling to plead her case. If she's not calling to plead her case then she's calling to try to get me to get her a lawyer. I'm not getting her shit!" he yelled, scaring me a little.

I touched his arm because he had balled up his fist and he was just blankly staring ahead now. I looked at his face and saw a single tear slide down his cheek and in that moment my heart ached so bad for this man who I had grown to know so quickly.

"I understand," I whispered.

"I just don't get it. How the fuck could she do something like that to our child. This shit has been fucking with me daily. I hate that woman's guts and I want to see her in a grave like the one she put our daughter in. I want that bitch to pay. She had no fucking right to take my child away from me. She had no right to do that shit! It doesn't matter what we had going on! This shit hurt!" he yelled before completely breaking down in front of me.

I didn't bother to tell him that I already knew his story. I didn't think it really mattered anyway. What mattered was that for some reason he felt like it was okay for him to open up to me. That meant more to me than he would probably ever know. I wrapped my arms around him as best as I could as he cried in my lap.

I knew he had probably been carrying this hurt for a long time and that was to be expected. I just wanted him to get it all out. I didn't care how long it took. The first step to healing was hurting and feeling the pain. The longer he waited to embrace the pain the longer it would take him to heal.

You could never get over a loss of someone close, but I wanted his soul to at least heal for his sake. I understood why his expression had changed so drastically now. Every time he got a call from his baby's mother he would be forced to face reality of what had happened. It didn't matter if he lived his day to day life acting like nothing had happened because when she called he realized that his worst fears had indeed happened. Out of the blue he sat up and then stood before walking straight out of the room. I heard a door slam and I didn't know what to do or say.

About an hour later he reappeared looking normal again. I could smell the scent of weed so I knew he had been smoking. I had been so worried about him that I had yelled his name out. He didn't reappear right then, he just yelled back that he was good. So, I was glad that he had finally came back out. I was starting to think that maybe he wanted to be left alone, but that was the last thing I was going to do.

"Are you alright?" I asked.

"I'm good. Don't worry about any of that. My fault, sometime the situation just gets the best of me. I'm good, trust me." he tried to brush the whole thing off and I didn't like that at all.

"Don't do that," I stood up and said, walking over to where he stood in front of the TV.

"What?"

"Don't apologize for showing your emotions. We're all human and we all have them. I know you're supposed to be this big tough guy or whatever who has all his shit together, but don't do that. It's okay to hurt, Kill. I can only imagine what you have been through and I know we're really just now getting to know each other, but you don't have to act in front of me. I thought you knew that. I'm here for you and you can take my word for that." I reached up and cuffed the side of his face.

His eyes were red and low from smoking, or maybe even crying, but the way he looked at me was indescribable. He didn't say anything, he just continued to look down at me and nodded his head. He brought his forehead down to mine and just rested it there. We stared at each other a little longer before he gently kissed my lips full on, taking my breath away. He pulled away faster than I wanted him to.

"Thank you," he muttered. I couldn't say anything back if I wanted to. I was still in a daze from his sensual kiss.

Another hour flew by quickly and we were snuggled up on his couch watching Netflix. After the kiss nothing more happened. He just grabbed my hand and pulled me down on the couch with him before turning on Netflix. We were watching some funny movie and I was really enjoying my time with him. Things just flowed smoothly, and nothing was forced with us. We didn't try to figure out what was going on between us but instead we just went with the flow and I liked that a lot.

"Cadence," Kill suddenly said.

"Yes?" I asked and looked up at him.

"Did you already know about my situation before tonight?"

"How did you know?" I asked, giving myself away.

"I can read people, baby girl. It's what I do. When I started talking about my child you didn't pry for more information and you didn't look too shocked, but I could tell you felt bad for me. Let me guess, Tehani told you?"

"She did, I'm sorry."

"Don't be sorry. You can't help that your friend has to tell everything she knows it's cool, but look I just want to say this. Whenever you're ready to open up to me about what's going on with you, I'll be ready to listen."

A huge lumped formed in my throat. "H-h-how do you figure something is going on with me?"

"I just know and like I said when you're ready to open up about it, I'll be here."

He started back watching the movie after saying that, but I couldn't focus on the movie much after he said what he said. I just stared at the screen and got lost in my thoughts. Would I ever be ready to open up to him about what I was running from? That was one question I didn't know the answer to.

Tehani

"One virgin daiquiri for you," I said before placing a drink down in front of Cadence on the coffee table. "And one daiquiri loaded down with liquor for you." I placed the other drink down in front of Andrea. I walked back to the kitchen to grab my drink and then joined the girls back in the living room. We were having a girl's night at my place.

Two more weeks had passed by and much hadn't changed. Cadence was still spending a lot of time with Kill and I thought that was good for her. She was still waking up in the middle of the night screaming and that had me worried. Kill still hadn't found out shit and Cadence was refusing to open up to me about her home life. She had been here for a whole month now and it seemed like she was limiting what she told me, which wasn't much.

Of course, I loved her like a sister, and I didn't want to stress her out by constantly prying. I knew stress was the last thing she needed being pregnant and all. Hell, I had problems of my own. Keef was sending more and more people my way to buy guns. I mean the money was great, but the problem came in with keeping a constant gun supply. The guns were going quicker than I could get them in. It's like as soon as I got a batch of crates they would be gone.

When Keef's people brought the guns in they would always tell me how long it would be before they got their hands on more. This time it was going to be a whole fucking month and I had already sold out my used gun crates AND even my new gun crates. The used guns usually sold faster because they were cheaper than the new ones. I had mentioned this dilemma to Keef three times already since he started sending all the new customers my way. His dumbass didn't see the problem at all. He was such a small-minded nigga and it was starting to drive me nuts I swear.

I told him that we needed to find a new connect for the guns because we didn't have time to be waiting when there was money to be made. I thought after I said the last part he would be all for finding us a new connect. I mean everything was about money with him, so I just knew what I had said would be like music to his ears. WRONG! That nigga told me that his loyalty remained with the connect that he already had. Not only did he say that, but he felt like we were getting the guns for a perfect price since we were pocketing so much of the money. The shit was plain out stupid, and I didn't get him.

What was the point of him running his fucking mouth and bringing in all the new customers if his people couldn't even keep us supplied? The shit was ass backward, but that was okay. For the last few weeks I had been working on a plan of my own and it wouldn't be long until everything came into play. I was going to mention it to Keef when he called and if he wasn't on board I would just do the shit without him. I was the one making all the moves out here. I don't give a shit if he was the one sending me all the customers.

We were supposed to be a team and if he couldn't make the right decisions for us then I would! The fuck was he going to do about it? At the end of the day he ate if I allowed him to eat, because guess what? If I didn't put that money on his books… his ass didn't eat. He needed me, and I knew it. That's why I did me out in these streets now because I was the motherfucking boss. I just played my cards right and I would continue to do so. Even if it meant hiding shit from Keef. Hey, that's what I was best at anyway.

"What the hell are you over there thinking about? I've been talking for the last fifteen minutes and ain't nobody heard shit I said. Cadence's ass ain't even touch her drink or nothing. She just fell asleep that quick. She sleep, you zoned the fuck out. Oh, I know it's time for me to go. It's barely even ten at night and look what y'all doing." Andrea's fussing brought me right out of my thoughts and back to reality.

"Drea, don't trip. Cadence is pregnant so you already know sleep is her best friend. Plus, she already don't sleep that good at night as it is."

"Well, at least she got an excuse. What's your excuse for zoning out on me because I know I ain't boring?"

"Girl, I just got a lot on my mind."

"So in other words you were thinking about Keef? Just say that shit or was you thinking about Jaydon… the coochie licker?" Andrea stuck out her long tongue and started wiggling it around.

"Shut up, you just mad because Boston won't lick on that pussy of yours."

"Bruh, don't even remind me. I'm the side chick so he can't be licking on my pussy. At least that's what he's always preaching. Yet, he can shove his dick deep in me with no protection. I'm not buying that shit. If you ask me he can't eat no coochie."

I cracked up laughing at Andrea's craziness as my phone started to ring. When I saw it was Keef calling I put up a finger signaling for her to hold on. She shook her head nope and mouthed that she was leaving. I knew she was just itching to leave anyway. She always had somewhere to be, and she stayed running off.

"Be safe," I said as she made her way to the front door. "Hey, baby." I answered my phone.

"Ay where you at?" Keef yelled into the phone. He stayed yelling like I couldn't hear him or some shit.

"I'm at the crib. Why what's up?"

I looked over at Cadence and she was still sleeping. I relaxed a little. I still hadn't told her that I sold guns for a living, so I guess she wasn't the only one hiding something. I really wasn't hiding shit from her though. All she had to do was ask and I would tell her, but she hadn't asked so I figured she didn't want to know.

"Ay, Kocaine, who outside the door?" Keef asked the nigga he shared a cell with.

"Everything is everything, homie. Go ahead," I heard Kocaine say back.

"Bae, listen to what the fuck I'm about to tell you and don't say shit until I'm finished talking, just listen."

"I got a feeling I'm not about to like whatever it is that you about to say." I rolled my eyes, instantly getting annoyed. I had some shit to run by him and I just knew that whatever he was going to say was going to fuck up everything I already had planned.

"What I say, Tehani?"

"Fine, I'm listening."

"You know how I been trying to bring in more business by telling motherfuckers in here to tell their peoples about our gun business, right?"

"Yes." I looked down at my stiletto rainbow nails and waited for the part that I wasn't going to like.

"Well, that shit has backfired in a major way. Somebody been running their mouth to the fucking police. I have a pretty good idea who it is too. It got to be that Chan nigga. He wanted to put his people on and have them buy some guns from us, but the nigga been talked to much for my liking, so I told his ass I ain't know what he was talking about. Ever since then the nigga been looking at me funny. Not only that, he been getting food from all kind of restaurants brought in to him."

"What does that have to do with anything?"

"Baby, when the correctional officers start bringing motherfuckers food from the outside it can only mean one or two things."

"Which is what, Keef?"

"The nigga could be paying the officer to do it, but I know that ain't the case because I ain't never seen Chan buy shit in this bitch. So that means the motherfucker gotta' be snitching. He ain't know shit else to tell so to get back at me he started telling the cops whatever they wanted to hear. Kocaine just got word about this shit tonight."

"You so fucking stupid, Keef. I knew you running your mouth so much couldn't be good. It doesn't really matter though because my crates for the month already sold out. Now I'm having to wait on your people to bring me more. That's why I told you we need a new connect. It looks like we gone have to get a new one anyway because it probably won't be long before the old connect gets busted with motherfuckers running their mouth and shit. This is a fucking gun business not a cookie baking business you shouldn't have been talking so much to start with!"

"Ay, watch your fucking mouth, for real. You testing a nigga right now and you already know I don't like to be tested. Plus, you sound stupid as fuck so shut the hell up and listen while I let you know what's about to go on in the upcoming weeks. My man Kocaine getting out in two weeks to be exact."

"What does that have to do with anything?"

"Shit is too hot right now for you to be running the business. You my girl, Tehani. When shit starts to get ugly like this it's my job to take control and make all of the decisions."

"But you in jail," I said before I knew it.

"It don't fucking matter! Shut down shop and don't sell shit else. When Kocaine gets out he is going to take over the business. I know it's gone be hard for you to do because you love to run shit, but you have to fall back."

"Fall back and be broke? Nigga, are you stupid? We started this shit together, you and me, not no damn Kocaine. So please tell me how is it that he's just going to up and run shit now? Nah, I'm not even feeling that, and did you not hear a thing I said? Shop been shut down because your weak ass gun connect ain't got shit for us!"

"You better watch your fucking mouth before I send Kocaine home to do more than just take over a business. Stop playing with me, Tehani, and another thing."

"What now!"

"Is everything okay?" Cadence slowly sat up and looked at me.

"Oh yeah, girl. Everything is cool. I'm sorry if I woke you from yelling. I was just about to go in my room."

"No, it's fine, I need to go get in the bed anyway. Goodnight." She stood up and made her way down the hall to her room.

"Did you hear what I said, Tee?" Keef quizzed.

"No."

"I said Kocaine been locked up since he was fifteen—"

"So what the fuck that nigga know about running a business?" I went off.

"You real close to pissing me off, real talk. For the last time shut the fuck up! Now like I was saying. He been locked up since he was fifteen. He don't have anywhere to go. He got a sister up north that's taking care of his daughter, but he can't afford to make it up that way right now. I need you to get a room ready for him."

"Get a room ready for him for what?" This motherfucker was tripping now. How the hell was I supposed to do me with one of his lil' homies around?

"He gone stay there until he gets enough money for his own spot."

"Like hell you say!"

"This shit ain't up for debate."

"Why we just can't give him some money to get a spot, Keef?"

"Because he a grown ass man and he not just gone take no money from me. Plus, this works out better for everybody and he can make sure you straight just in case this shit gets ugly with the police."

"Oh, but he gone take a place to stay though?"

"It's not up for debate! I have to go now, the police about to do their nightly rounds. I love you."

Before I could protest or say anything else he hung up the phone. I just couldn't believe this shit. I didn't even get a chance to tell him about my plans, but I was glad that I didn't now. Bringing someone else in to run the business was stupid. I don't give a fuck if the police had been tipped off. Bringing someone else in meant splitting our money with another person and I wasn't feeling that at all. Kocaine could have Keef's business because as of tonight I was going into business by my damn self and wasn't shit going to stop me!

Andrea

I pulled up to the boat dock about fifteen minutes later than I was scheduled to arrive. That's why I had tried to turn down Tehani's invite to girl's night. Don't get me wrong, I loved to chill with her and Cadence, but I had some important business to take care of. For the last few months I had gotten involved in some shit that could cause me to do major jail time if I wasn't careful, but that was the thing, I was careful, so I wasn't even tripping. I was about to open my door to get out of the car when my phone started vibrating in the cup holder. I was going to ignore it until I saw it was my sister Marsha calling.

"What is it, Marsh?" I questioned, agitated by her call.

"Where you at, man? I been at the crib all evening waiting on your stinking ass. It ain't no food in this bitch and if I remember correctly you said you was going to go grocery shopping today. Oh, and what the fuck we gone do about all these damn rats that keep getting in the apartment? Them lil' traps you put out ain't doing shit. It'll kill one or two, but at this point we gone need more than that. Or I'mma start shooting these little fuckers heads off."

"Marsha, I'm going to handle it and I'll bring you something home to eat. I have to go!"

I hung up the phone and got out of my car after pulling my hood down over my head. I looked all around as I made my way to the edge of the dock. I was about to step on the yacht to knock on the little door when it came flying open.

"You're late. This will be your last time doing business with me," the guy who had opened the door said. He was mugging me, and I mugged his ass back. I didn't care how important he felt like he was. He was doing the same shit as me.

"My last time? This is my first time being late. I got tied up, you tripping now. I need this extra income to get my sister and I somewhere to stay. Our current apartment is in no shape for us to be living in."

"What did you do with the other money you've been getting paid?"

"Shit, I went shopping. I was going to use this money from tonight to at least put a down payment on something."

"Look, that's not my problem. Like I said this will be your last night. I have other deliveries to make and you've held me up. The only reason I waited is because of the person the package is going to. Now, come on so I can carry this shit to your trunk."

"I don't need you to carry a damn thing to my trunk. I can do it myself and I tell you that every time we meet up."

"Well, this will be the last time." He walked back in the inside of the yacht. When he reappeared, he had three duffel bags in his hands that he dropped at my feet on the dock.

"You can't be serious," I said as I leaned down to pick up the bags.

"I am serious." That was all he said before the yacht started moving away from the dock. I just stood there in the dark and watched the yacht sail off. I blew out a frustrated breath as I went back to my car with the duffel bags. I quickly put them in my trunk before jumping in my car and speeding off.

I was pissed. All my money from the diner was already tied up in bills. I had just got paid yesterday and that whole check was already almost gone. I had planned to use the money, from picking up drugs, on groceries and a down payment on this place I had been looking at for Marsha and I. Our current apartment had gotten infested with rats and those little motherfuckers had started chewing through all of my shoes. I knew it was time for us to relocate then, but I could only afford to do so much at a time.

I finally pulled in front of my apartment complex and parked my car. I looked all around before getting out of the car. I quickly went to the trunk and grabbed all of the duffel bags out before slamming it back closed. It was a good thing that I was in shape because there was no way in hell I would have been able to lift those bags by myself if I didn't have a little muscle. That's why I hated for people to underestimate me. I may have looked weak as hell, but in actuality I was strong as shit. Lucky, for me my arms weren't all bulky, but the muscles were there.

"What's in the bags?" Marsha asked as soon I walked through the front door.

"Not shit for you. Mind your business," I snapped.

"Damn, I just asked a question. Where is my food at? Obviously, it's not in those damn duffel bags."

"Let me put these heavy ass bags up and then we can go and get something to eat."

I walked through the living room to get to my room. As soon as I got in there I dropped the bags on the floor and opened the closet door. I shoved all the bags inside one by one before returning to the living room. Marsha had just slipped on her shoes when I walked in. She squinted her eyes at me and crossed her arms over her chest. I knew she was about to get on my everlasting nerves, and I was nowhere near in the mood for her shit.

Basically, I had just got fired from the job that was paying me the most. The money from the diner would never be enough to get us out of this small ass apartment. I mean yeah, I could take the money I would get paid for this delivery and put a down payment on something, but then what after that? I would never be able to keep up with the payments without making drug deliveries. I mentally cursed myself out for blowing all of the other money. I could be so irresponsible at times and now the shit was costing me. Big time.

"You're up to something," Marsha finally said.

"Save it and come the hell on." I walked to the door and opened it before practically sprinting out. There was no need though because Marsha was right on my heels. "Did you lock the front door?" I asked as we neared the car.

"What's the point? If someone wants something out of that raggedy ass apartment, they're stupid as fuck."

"Did you lock the fucking door or not?" I stopped dead in my tracks and questioned.

"Yeah, what the hell is up with you tonight?"

"Just get in the car."

Once we both were inside, I started the car up and pulled out into the streets. Marsha was saying something, but I wasn't paying her much attention. I got lost in my thoughts quick. I thought back to a few months ago when I first got introduced to the drug world. I had always known about it or dealt with guys who lived that type of lifestyle, but I had never been involved in the mix personally.

It all started one night after I had met up with Boston at our usual hotel room. I was complaining about money to him in hopes that he would break me off. It never worked out that way with Boston. You see, Boston claimed to be in love with his wife. That meant he wasn't going to be lacing another bitch's pockets with money. That was one of his rules right along with the rule about him not eating my pussy. If he loved his wife so much why did he even bother with me? This pussy was bomb that's why. Unfortunately, it wasn't bomb enough to make him cough up the dough though. He would fuck me and that would be it.

Well, on that night I guess my complaining got to him or maybe I threw the pussy on him a little better than usual because he cracked and decided to help me. Instead of giving me money flat out he told me I could pick up deliveries for him. The only thing was, I couldn't tell anyone. Not even Kill knew that Boston was allowing me to pick up their drugs. Boston was paying the guy on the boat to not open his mouth about it. Now that I think about it, he had probably been waiting for a reason to get rid of me. Bitch ass nigga was scared of Kill and couldn't take keeping our secret.

Now I was the one suffering because he ain't have enough heart to go against his boss. That was okay though because if I had to go down, I was going to take whoever the hell I could with me. That included Boston too because all he had to do was give me money. Yet, he wanted to act like he couldn't do so. Right then and there I decided that I wouldn't be delivering shit. Those drugs back in my closet was officially mine. I would sell them and then get as far away from this fucking city as I could. I knew it was a big risk to take, but it was one I was willing to make.

When I snapped back into reality Marsha was yelling for me to turn into a fast food restaurant. I whipped right in and drove up to the drive-thru. We placed our order and then we drove to the next window to pay for our food and get it. I was glad that Marsha had finally stopped bitching. I know that I had forgot to stop and get her food on the way home, but I was so focused on getting those drugs out of my car that it had slipped my mind.

As soon as we got our food I sped back toward our apartment. About twenty minutes later we were pulling back up at our apartment complex and my fucking heart hit the floor. Our door was wide open. I knew what happened right away. I parked the car and my head dropped down to the steering wheel in defeat.

"Fuck… Fuck! Fuck! Fuck! Fuck! fuck!" I yelled.

"What the FUCK is wrong with you?" Marsha asked, trying to be cute. My head popped up so quick that I almost gave myself whiplash.

"Did you lock my fucking door before we left? And don't lie because I'm going to slap the shit out of you. I swear to god I am."

"No, I didn't lock the funky ass door." She hopped out the car with the food in her hands. I got out as well and took off running to our apartment.

As soon as I got inside I saw that everything had been flipped over. I went straight to my room. The closet door was wide open and of course all of the fucking duffel bags were gone. Someone had been watching me and as soon as we left they probably went straight in our shit. If Marsha had locked the fucking door my drugs may have never been taken. Then again, we lived in the fucking hood. They probably would have kicked the damn door down to get to those duffel bags. I had fucked up and I knew it. Not only did I not have the drugs, but I didn't have the money to escape either. I was fucked.

"What happened?" Marsha asked, standing in the doorway.

"Just get out!" I yelled and slammed my door shut in her face. *What the fuck was I going to do now?*

Killian

I was about to get ready to leave my office at the restaurant when there was a tap at the door. I immediately got annoyed because I was about to head to pick Cadence up for lunch. We couldn't hang out last night because she was having girl's night or some shit like that with her wild ass friends. Since Cadence was six months pregnant now they decided to have their girl's night at Tehani's instead of going out. That eased my mind because I didn't want Cadence at no club or no fucking bar. She didn't belong at either of those places while she was pregnant. She may not have been my girl, but that didn't mean she wouldn't be. Therefore, I wasn't going for none of that bullshit.

"Come in!" I yelled out. I stood up and waited for the person at my door to come in.

"Hey, it's me," Ambrysha said as she walked in.

"What can I do for you, Brysha?" I looked down at my Diamond Gold Rolex and then I looked back at her.

"Oh, I'm sorry. Were you about to head out?"

"Actually, I was, but what's up?"

"Did you see that Gordon was killed on the news?"

"Nah," I told her, walking around my desk.

"That's terrible. I wonder who could have done something like that."

"Don't know, don't care."

"It happened the same day he was fired. I just keep thinking that if he hadn't got fired on that particular day that he would have been here working and not at home. Then, he would have never been killed. It's so sad, it's just been on my mind."

"It's life. He was a fuck nigga. He probably was stealing from other people too and somebody just caught up with his ass. That's how that shit go."

"I guess." She looked at me funny and I already knew what she was thinking.

"I gotta' go and here's a tip for the future, baby girl, always mind the business that pays you. Have a good day and let me know if you need anything. I'll be gone for the rest of the day."

She nodded her head and turned to walk out of my office in a hurry. I followed behind her and locked my office up before going out the back exit. As soon as I got on the road my phone started to ring. I looked down and saw that it was Boston calling. I reached down and grabbed it right away.

"Talk to me."

"Kill, you're not going to like this shit," Boston said, not wasting time at all.

"I'm listening." I gripped the steering wheel tight because I knew the bullshit he was about to tell me was going to piss me the fuck off.

"Man, the pack ain't show the fuck up this morning."

"Where the fuck you at?"

"I'm at the crib. Ay—"

"I'm on the way," I said and hung up on his ass.

I stepped on the gas harder and flew all the way to his crib. It only took me ten minutes to get there and I was glad because I didn't want to be late to pick up Cadence. As usual business was popping up and getting in the way of our time together. It seemed like every time I was supposed to go and get her something popped up that I would have to handle before I got to her. I pulled into Boston's driveway and he was standing on the front porch smoking a backwood. I parked the car and hopped out.

"Damn my nigga, you got here quick as hell," Boston said as I walked up on the porch.

"You damn right I did. You know not to tell me no shit like that over the phone."

"That's my fuck up. This shit got me pissed the fuck off."

"What the hell happened? How the fuck my packs ain't show up this morning? They been showing up and you still been going to get them, right?"

"About that."

"What the fuck about it, Boston? We never make mistakes because we don't have room for that shit. So, what the fuck is there for you to say about that?" Boston was my homeboy and all, but I was good and ready to go all in his shit.

"Man, you know I'm all about my wife, but I like to keep me a little piece on the side or whatever."

"The fuck that got to do with anything my nigga?"

"My side chick had been complaining about having money problems for the longest and you know me, I'm not about to come up off that paper to no bitch but Destiny. Anyway, I figured I would put shawty on so she could make a little bread."

"Nah, nah, I know you not about to say what the fuck I think you about to say. I just know you not."

"Dawg, I swear to god I thought she could be trusted. I mean I got the bitch wrapped around my finger. Whatever I say go and she knows that. She's been picking up the packs from the boat dock for the last few months and she ain't never pulled no shit like this. I been calling her phone all morning and she hasn't answered once. She always answers the fucking phone even when she's at work. Now it's noon and the bitch still not picking up. That's when I just went ahead and called you because I know some shit going on. Fuck, I knew I shouldn't have showed no sympathy for that bitch!"

"Tell me this."

"What's up?" he asked, finally passing the blunt.

"Please tell me that the side chick you talking about wasn't Andrea?" He didn't even have to answer because the guilty expression on his face told me that it was. "Damn, Boston!"

"Don't trip, I'm going to find that bitch and get our shit. I just wanted to put you up on game about this shit."

"Look, I got somewhere to be, but I'm trusting you to fix this shit and fix it quick because if I don't get my packs or the profit for them…. Somebody is going to die."

I flicked the last bit of the blunt on the ground and turned to leave. I didn't have shit else to say to Boston until he fixed the problem that he had caused for us. Out of all the bitches in Miami it just ain't no way that motherfucker had decided to trust Andrea. The bitch was sleezy as they came and I was disappointed in my homeboy, but I was going to give him time to fix this shit before I got really violent.

Cadence

I stepped out of the shower and wrapped my towel around my body. I walked over to the foggy mirror and wiped it off as best as I could with my hand. I grabbed my eye drops off the countertop and squirted two drops in each eye. My eyes were blood shot red. I hadn't been getting much sleep lately due to my nightmares. I often woke up screaming my head off, sometime scaring my damn self. I would stay up for hours after a nightmare and as soon as I would get back to sleep the nightmare would happen all over again.

After I was done drying my body off, I sat on the toilet and rubbed lotion all over my body. I slipped on a red bra with the matching panties. I decided to wear a pair of dark blue jeggings with a red maternity tank top and a pair of red loafers. I applied the same color lipstick to my lips along with a little foundation and mascara. I pulled my hair down out of the high bun it was in and ran my hand through my long, wavy, black bundles.

Once I was done, I walked back to my bedroom. I felt my baby moving around a little and I touched my stomach and smiled. No matter how my child had been conceived I was going to love her unconditionally. She was a part of me, and she always would be. A tear rolled down my right cheek and I didn't even bother to wipe it away. Thinking about my situation always made me emotional. I sighed and walked over to the bed to grab my phone. Kill had sent a text that said he was ten minutes away.

I heard Tehani moving around out in the hallway and I thought back to last night. She thought I had been sleeping when she was on the phone talking to her boyfriend. I knew she had to be involved in some crazy shit, but I would have never thought that she was running a gun business. I didn't even have room to judge her. At least she was making money and she wasn't selling pussy or anything like that. My question was why was Kill buying guns if he was a businessman? That's what wasn't making sense to me.

"You okay?" I heard Tehani suddenly ask.

"Yeah, why what's up?" I looked up and smiled at her.

"I was knocking on your door, but you never said for me to come in. Then, when I walk in, you're in here all zoned out. What's on your mind?"

"Nothing, I'm fine. I'm waiting on Kill; he's taking me to lunch."

"Look at you blushing. I guess he's a good distraction from your problems?" she pried.

"Why does everyone think I'm having some kind of problems?"

"Because you don't hide it well. We can talk about it, Cady, maybe I can help." My phone dinged with a text from Kill saying that he had pulled up.

"Kill's here, let me get out here before he feels the need to come to the door." As soon as the words left my mouth we heard someone knocking on the door. "Told you! I'll be back later." I walked over to her and kissed her cheek before heading out of the room in a hurry.

I walked to the front door and opened it for Kill. As soon as he saw me his face lit up and mine did too. We just stared at each other and smiled like a couple of idiots. Yet, that didn't stop us from doing it. I heard Tehani walk up behind me and clear her throat.

"Will y'all make it official already and stop playing with each other? I'm so sick of this." She commented.

"And will you mind your business, nosey ass," Kill said, and I laughed.

"Now you know Tehani wouldn't be Tehani if she minded her own business."

"Whatever, Cady. You kids have fun. I have some business of my own to take care of anyway."

I laughed as I walked out of the house and closed the door behind me. Kill grabbed my hand and we went and got in the car. Once we were on the road and away from Tehani and her interrogation I relaxed.

"Wow," I said as we pulled up to the restaurant about thirty minutes later. You could see straight through the restaurant. It was made of glass and it was directly on the beach. The whole sight was something to gawk at.

"Close ya' mouth before I put my tongue in it," Kill said before hopping out of the car and then walking around to open my door. I just smiled at him as he leaned over me to unbuckle my seat belt. He grabbed my hand and helped me out the car.

When we made it inside Kill had the hostess sit us outside so we could see the ocean while we ate. As soon as I saw it I was instantly reminded of home. The memories were good at first until an image of blood and then fire popped up in my head. I just sat in my seat and stared at the water until the waitress walked over to take our drink orders. I was glad when she did because it pulled me out of my thoughts.

"You good?" Kill asked and I nodded my head.

"So what can I get for the two of you?" the waitress asked, smacking on her gum.

"Let me get some Jameson on the rocks and a Corona." Kill was the first to answer her.

"And for you, sweetheart?"

"A water will be fine."

"Alright, I'll be right back with that. When is the baby due? I know the two of you must be excited. Is this your first child?" she looked at us and asked. Kill looked uncomfortable as sadness washed over his face. I knew his thoughts had instantly went to his daughter. I quickly spoke up so he wouldn't have to.

"This will be my first child. I have three more months to go."

"Nice, well congrats you guys." She smiled at us before walking off to get our drinks.

"Thanks," Kill looked at me and said.

"No problem, you okay?"

"Yeah, it just gets hard when I think about my situation."

"I know, but I'm here for you." I reached across the table to grab his hands.

"I appreciate it."

We grew quiet for a little bit and then I let his hands go to look over the menu and he done the same. The waitress finally came back over and placed our drinks on the table. She took our order and then walked away again. I was starving and my baby was kicking me, so I guess she was just as hungry as I was. Kill had drunk his Jameson on the rocks in one gulp and was looking for the waitress again so he could order another cup. I guess his nerves had started getting the best of him after he started thinking about his daughter. I felt so bad for him and all I wanted to do was take that pain away, but I knew it would take time. When Kill spotted the waitress walking by he waved her over and told her to get him another glass and then he looked at me.

"You ready to eat?"

"You know I am," I giggled.

"Me too, I've been ready to come eat with you all day."

"Well, who better to eat with than a pregnant person?"

"Right. I know you greedy as shit."

"I am not."

"Yeah okay."

"Whatever."

"There was something I wanted to talk with you about though."

"What's up?" I asked, taking a sip of my water.

"I wanted to get your advice on something."

"Okay."

"I was thinking about opening up my first hotel in California. I know that's where you're from so I wanted to know how good you think business would be there?"

"Well, it's California so of course business would be great, but what's going to set your hotel apart from the rest?"

"I'm glad you asked that." He smiled at me big and I was glad to see his smile. I knew he was relaxed again, and I was happy for that.

"Tell me."

"I want my hotel to be really futuristic like. I already know it's going to have a huge ass casino in it like some Las Vegas type of shit. I also plan to make everything easier for my guests though. Instead of having a front desk with someone behind it doing all the work I want everything to be computer operated. I've been talking with this technician from California and he thinks my ideas or great and it won't be too hard to do. So instead of going to the front desk to check in you would go to this screen and be able to punch all of your information in. After you swipe your card or pay with cash the machine will spit out your room key with the number to your room on it. I mean of course I'll have actual workers too just in case the machine malfunctions or something, but the objective is to make it to where we wouldn't have to worry about that."

"Nice, but what about a bellhop? How could your guest get their luggage to their room if they didn't want to carry it?"

"You're asking all the right questions. I'll have robots as the bellhops that would take your luggage to your room for you and serve drinks to my guest as soon as they come in."

"I like that a lot! I think California would be a great place for your hotel. You gone have all the famous people coming there."

"That's the point," Kill said as the waitress brought our food out. As soon as my plate hit the table in front of me I started digging in. I was not playing when I said that me and my baby were ready to eat. I looked across the table and Kill was just looking at me with an amused expression on his face.

"What?" I asked with a mouth full of food.

"Nothing, don't let me stop you. Keep bussing that shit down, I like it."

"I'm glad you do because I surely wasn't about to stop eating."

"I would never ask you no shit like that, but I do have something else to ask you."

"Go ahead."

"I actually have to go to California this weekend to meet up with the technician I have working on all of this shit. I also have to meet up with a realtor to see where I want my hotel to be or if I want to have it built from the ground up. I was thinking that you could come with me since you're familiar with the area. Oh and I enjoy having you around, you make me feel better."

I couldn't respond to Kill right away. I just sat there holding my fork in midair. Going back to California was the last thing I wanted to do. I searched my mind high and low for an excuse of why I couldn't go to California with him. I honestly didn't have one, except for I didn't want what I was running from to catch up with me. Of course I couldn't tell him that though. I had to make myself take a deep breath and then I plastered a fake smile across my face.

"I would love to go with you," I said as my heart was pounding in my chest.

"Really? Why you look so worried about it though?"

"Oh, it's nothing. I just haven't been home in a month now that's all." I took a bite of the food that was on my fork and looked down at my plate.

"Are you scared you will run into your baby's father? If so you don't have shit to worry about. I'll protect you, Cadence. I know we never talked much about that, but I got you."

"That means a lot to me. We just left off on bad terms. I didn't even tell him I was leaving, I just left. I haven't talked to him since."

"Do you mind me asking what made you do that?"

"I'd rather not talk about that. What we had is over and I'm just trying to move on with my life."

"I can understand that, no pressure."

"I guess since we will be going back to California though I can go to my doctor's appointment since you will be with me. It's kind of funny because I have one on Friday. I haven't been to the doctor since I've been here, and I know I need to go. I've just being dealing with a lot of personal stuff."

"Like I told you before, when you're ready to open up to me I'm here. You're definitely going to that doctor's appointment though. You can't be missing appointments when you're pregnant, Cadence. Something could be going on with the baby and you wouldn't even know. If you want, we can get them to fax your information here to one of the doctor's offices. Or we can keep flying back and forth, but what you're not going to do is miss another appointment. Got it?"

"Yes, Doctor Kill, I got it." I laughed.

"Cool, what time is your appointment Friday?"

"It's at eleven."

"Okay, we will fly out early that morning and go straight to your appointment from there. Is that okay with you?"

"Yeah, that sounds good."

We finished eating our food and then Kill paid the bill before we headed back to the car. On the ride home we listened to the music, but we didn't talk much. He finally pulled back up in front of Tehani's house and parked his car. I wanted to ask him what a man like him would need with a crate of guns, but I wasn't stupid, and something told me that he was involved in the streets. Yet, that didn't make me want to stop hanging with him. He was my security blanket and the feeling he gave me when he was around wasn't one I was willing to let go of so quickly.

"I enjoyed lunch with you."

"I enjoyed lunch with you too. Thanks for taking me," I said and then opened my car door. Before I could get out he grabbed my hand and I turned back around to face him. When I did he leaned over the seat and pulled me closer to him. I closed my eyes and allowed him to kiss me. Once he pulled away I could still feel my lips tingling from the kiss.

"I'll call you later on alright?" he asked as I got out of the car.

"Okay." I smiled at him and then slammed my door shut before walking up on the porch.

I walked over to the porch swing and took a seat. I watched as Kill pulled out of Tehani's yard and left. Once his car was so far down the street that I couldn't see it anymore I pulled out my phone to call my mother. She had been on my mind a lot lately and I just wanted to call and check on her. I dialed her number and then waited for her to answer. It took her longer than usual to answer but she finally did.

"Hey baby, I'm so glad to hear from you. I was starting to get worried sweetie. You know better than to go that long without at least calling."

"I know, Mama, and I'm sorry. I came to Florida to get away for a little bit and clear my head. I'm here with Tehani. Do you remember her?"

"Of course I remember my second child. How is she doing now? How did the two of you get back in touch?"

"She's doing really good and remember I told you we had found each other on Facebook."

"That's right. I'm glad you're okay and with someone who will watch out for you. I know you have to take time for yourself sometime but baby you have to take care of you and that baby as well. I was so worried I had called your doctor's office and they told me that you hadn't been to any of you doctor's appointments last month. What's up with that?"

"Yeah, I know and that's my fault. I have a doctor's appointment Friday and I'll be flying back to go to it. I was calling to tell you that I wanted to stop by and see you. I'm not going to be in town long when I come back."

"Sweetie, are you sure everything is alright? Why are you going back to Florida when your life and Lennox is here? That child has been worried sick about you. Why would you leave and not tell him where you were going?"

"Ma, I will explain everything to you when I come back, okay?"

"Alright, but do you want to talk to him before you go?"

"He's there now?"

"Yes, he's in the living room and I'm in the kitchen. He's been here every day since you left."

"Ma, listen I have to go. Do me a favor and don't tell him you talked to me, okay?"

"Okay, but what is going on—"

"I love you, see you soon," I said and then hung up the phone.

My heart was pounding in my chest just thinking about Lennox. He had been blowing my phone up until I blocked his number. He was the last person I wanted to see or talk to and I only hoped that my mother listened to what I had said and didn't tell him we had talked. I took a deep breath and then got up from the swing to go in the house. I needed to lay down for a little while and sort the mess that I had left back home out in my head. Maybe going back to California wasn't such a good idea after all, but I didn't know what else to do.

Lennox

"Was that Cade you were just talking to on the phone?" I walked into the kitchen and asked Cadence's mother. She spun around so quick to look at me.

"Oh, no, no that wasn't Cady. That was the doctor's office calling to see if I had heard anything from her since she missed two appointments last month."

"Why would they call to ask you that instead of calling me? I'm her boyfriend, not you."

"Yes, well I'm her mother and they probably didn't want to stress you more than you already are."

"Yeah… you're probably right," I said, staring at her for a long second. She was just like her daughter, neither of them could tell a decent lie.

What she didn't know was that as soon as she had gone into the kitchen to answer the phone I had picked up the phone that was in the living room. I had heard their whole entire phone conversation and I was furious. Cadence's mother lying straight to my face was only making me angrier. I knew she had to know more than what she was telling me. Her fucking daughter had ran off to Florida with my child in her stomach and she didn't think that was something I needed to know? I squeezed my fist tightly.

"Are you alright, Lennox?"

"Actually, I'm not." I was getting ready to do something that I would probably regret later, but her daughter wasn't here for me to take my anger out on and her husband wasn't here either. Someone was going to have to feel the pain that I was feeling, and it was going to be her. She visually started to tremble a little and look uncomfortable.

"I know this is, uhm, I know it's tough for you. Bu… but everything is going to be okay."

"Is that right?" I asked, stepping closer to her.

"Yes, I'm sorry, Lennox, but I'm going to have to ask you to leave. I don't like the way you're looking at me and you're starting to make me uncomfortable," she said all of that in one breath. Before I could do or say anything else my cellphone started to ring in my pocket. I pulled it out and then held up one finger after I saw who was calling me.

"What's up?" I asked my partner.

"Man, where are you at right now? You need to get to your brother's beach house immediately. Something awful has happened."

"I'm on my way!" I yelled into the phone and then hung it up. "Unfortunately, work calls. I'll be in touch," I told Cadence's mother before sprinting out the kitchen and back to the living room to go out the front door.

Cadence and my brother both had been missing for a month in total now. I hadn't heard anything from either of them. Now that I knew Cadence was in Florida I was wondering what could have been going on at my brother's beach house. He didn't go there often, and my mind was racing as I jumped in my car and sped to his beach house. Cadence's parents didn't live far from my brother's beach house, so it only took me ten minutes flat to get there.

I parked my car and hopped out. I saw my boss and partner standing together and looking at the house. There was an ambulance out front along with a good many cop cars. I stared at my brother's beach house as I walked over to my boss and partner. When my boss saw me his eyes got big and then he looked straight at my partner.

"I thought I made myself clear when I said for no one to call Lennox!" he yelled at him.

"I'm sorry boss man, but he needed to see this," my partner Alfred said.

"What the hell happened here?" I asked.

"Lennox we're going to get to the bottom of everything, but I think it's best if you leave and head on home," my boss said, placing his hand on my shoulder and looking me in my eyes.

"He wasn't in there was he?"

"Their searching the house now, or at least what's left of it."

My brother's house had been burned down. You could see straight through it. I didn't know what had happened or when it had caught fire, but the house was in a secluded area. He only had one neighbor and they didn't even live in town. They only came in town to vacation, so it made sense that his home hadn't been discovered sooner.

"When did it burn down? Is his house the only thing that caught on fire?" I inquired.

"Yes, it looks like his house was the only one that caught on fire. I don't know when the fire started, but it had to be no later than a month ago from the look of things. We still wouldn't have known if his neighbors hadn't came to town and saw it. They called the police as soon as they spotted it and then the cops called us. We didn't want to call you until we knew exactly what was going on. It's a good thing the fire didn't escalate more, or everything down here would have caught on fire too. It look like whoever started the fire had tried to put it out, but we're not sure yet."

"Who is that? Who is that they're bringing out?" I asked as someone was being carried out in a body bag. I didn't even wait for a response. I took off to where the body was being carried out. "Who is this?" I asked once I made it over to where the officers and everyone else was standing.

"Unzip the bag," the cop told one of the coroners and he stopped and pulled the zipper down so that I could see. When I looked at the person they were all burnt up, but I knew for a fact that it was my brother who had been burned inside of his home.

"Fuck!" I yelled, before storming away and walking right back over to where my boss and partner was standing at. "You fucking knew he was dead didn't you! You knew, you guys had to investigate the scene before they could take that body out and you didn't even tell me! What the hell is wrong with you!" I yelled in my bosses face.

"Okay, son, I think you need to head on home now. We didn't tell you because we knew you'd respond like this. We're thinking maybe he was killed before the house was burned down because of the way we found him. Let us do our job and we will get to the bottom of all of this. Take a few weeks off or however long you need." My boss tried to rub my shoulder again, but I slapped his hand away from me and ran back to my car.

"I'm sorry, man!" I heard Alfred yell as I got into my vehicle. I started it up and sped off.

Something just wasn't right to me. Cadence and my brother both had disappeared around the same time. Now my brother was dead, and she was all the way in fucking Florida. I didn't know the story behind everything but the sooner I found Cadence would be the better. I knew for a fact that she was planning to come back Friday and when she did… I would be waiting for her. She was going to tell me everything I wanted to know, or my brother wasn't going to be the only one being carried in a body bag and I meant that shit!

Jaydon

"What's good, Boston?" I asked slapping hands with him before I walked inside of his home. He closed the door behind him and then I followed him down to the basement so we could talk and smoke a blunt.

"Man, ain't shit good right about now," he said once we we're seated. I pulled a pack of cigars out my pocket and got ready to roll a blunt.

"Why you say that?"

"I guess you haven't talked to Kill?"

"Nah, you know he stay up under that girl that's visiting Tehani."

"You met her?"

"Yeah she cool."

"Shit I should have figured that much if he's taking her to California with him."

"Right, when is he leaving out again?"

"The first thing in the morning and then he will be back Sunday if not sooner. That's not the problem though."

"What the hell is the problem? Ain't nobody told me shit about a problem."

"Haven't nobody told you anything because I have from now until Kill gets back to fix this shit."

"Fix what?" I asked as I finished up rolling the blunt. I pulled out my lighter and lit the tip.

"I fucked up, Jay. I fucked up bad. You know how I was fucking with Andrea right?"

"Yeah."

"One day this broad got to talking about how she ain't have no money and how she couldn't do shit. Blah blah blah and some more shit about her raggedy ass apartment. You know me, I'm not about to give no bitch no money. I don't care how good that pussy might be hitting. I felt bad for her though and I really just wanted her to shut the fuck up so I could hit. Me being me, I tossed the bitch a bone and told her she could do deliveries for us. Her job was to pick the drugs up and then deliver them to me the next morning. Well she ain't show up with our shit the other morning like she was supposed to. I panicked and called Kill to put him up on game. The nigga was cooler about it than I expected but if I don't get this shit handled all hell is going to break loose. Now I can't even find the fucking bitch!"

"She left her crib?"

"Hell yeah, and she hasn't been to work either. I think that bitch ran off on our asses."

"Nah, I know she can't be that bold."

"Then where the fuck is our shit at and where the hell have she ran off to?"

"Ion know, dawg. Here, hit this shit you need to relax." I passed the blunt I had been smoking on over to Boston.

"This shit is gone be on me. I regret ever getting caught up with that snake ass bitch. Yo' ass need to leave Tehani alone too. You see this cheating shit ain't getting us nowhere."

"Now you tripping, ain't shit about to make me stop fucking with that sexy ass motherfucker. Your ass is married so you had no business fucking with Andrea to start with. Maybe this yo' Karma or some shit."

"Nigga what the hell you know about some damn Karma. This ain't no Karma, that bitch just fucked me over! I'm not about to let this shit get me demoted when I'm Kill's right hand man. I called you over here to see if you had saw Andrea with Tehani or some shit. We gotta' get those fucking drugs back or I'm going to have to come out of my own pockets just to fix this shit. I can't do that man. You know how much that shit is worth after it's been flipped? That's going to take a huge chunk out of my pockets, and I got a fucking family to feed."

"Damn, I see where you getting at with all of this. I'll let you know if I hear anything and I'll be on the lookout for that bitch my damn self. She's crossed the wrong ones. Don't even sweat it, we will have this shit all figured out before Sunday."

"Word, I appreciate you helping a nigga."

"You know we all ride together…"

"And gone die together," Boston finished the sentence and we slapped hands.

"Let me get up out of here though. Madden has been on my ass ever since that night we ran into Andrea and Tehani's messy asses. I swear she would put a collar around my damn neck if she could."

"As she should." Boston laughed.

"Whatever, at least I'm not the nigga that's married, but you know I'm not the one to judge."

"Yeah, yeah, yeah. Let me walk to the door and make sure you not trying to fuck my bitch," Boston joked.

"I hit that shit in high school. Destiny got some good shit too." I laughed and then smirked at Boston.

"Nigga stop it."

He put the rest of the blunt out and then we headed upstairs. He knew I had never fucked with Destiny a day in my damn life, but we liked to fuck with each other for the hell of it. When we made it to the door we slapped hands one more time and I headed out. I couldn't believe that Andrea had ran off on the plug. That was one brave bitch, but I refused to let my homeboy go down because of her ass. Kill was our boy, but he didn't play when it came to his money and in the end someone was going to have to pay for all of this shit.

Tehani

It was finally Friday and I was standing in the doorway of Cadence's room as she finished packing her bags. It was going on five in the morning and Kill was on his way to pick her up. She had been acting a little strange ever since she told me that Kill wanted her to go to California with him and I thought that was weird. I knew for a fact that it had something to do with going back home. That told me that my suspicions had been right all along, and something had happened back home that she was running away from. She had been avoiding having the conversation with me, but I was going to get some answers out of her before she left this morning.

"All done," Cadence said, zipping up her suitcase. She was about to try to pull the suitcase off the bed but I walked over and done it for her and then lifted up the handle so she would be able to roll it out of her room when Kill came.

"I told you it would have been easier if you had packed your things last night. Then you could have gotten a little extra sleep this morning."

"Yeah, I know, but I wanted to try to get some sleep."

"About that, sit down for a minute and you might as well not even try to give me a lame excuse. We're having this talk now." I sat down on the bed and patted the spot next to me.

"I think Kill is here."

"No he's not and if he is he can come in and wait. Sit down, Cady, seriously."

"Fine." She sighed.

"Some nights you wake up in the middle of the night screaming so loud that you wake me up." I jumped straight into the conversation. There was no need to beat around the bush. I had been trying to have this conversation with her for weeks now.

"I'm so sorry, I didn't know I had been waking you up out of your sleep. I keep having these bad nightmares."

"No, it's okay. I just want you to tell me what's going on with you. We both know that you are hiding something from me. I mean I know we hadn't seen each other in a while before a month ago, but you can trust me. Whatever it is bothering you maybe I can help some kind of way."

"You don't understand, Tee. No one can help me with my situation."

"Is it your baby's father?"

"Yes, but then no."

"I don't understand that, Cady. Please just tell me exactly what happened before you came here. I promise I won't say not one word to anybody." Cadence looked at me for a second and then she started to cry.

I wrapped my arms around her and held her as tight as I could without squeezing her stomach too hard. She broke down in my arms and started to get choked up as she tried to explain her story. I had to shush her and tell her to take a minute. After a couple of minutes passed by of her crying she finally lifted her head back up and took a deep breath. I knew whatever it was had to be serious for it to make her break down like that. I quickly braced myself for whatever it was that she was about to say.

"Tee, I was raped six months ago. The guy that did it tried to do it to me again. He came to my house and forced me to leave with him just so he could do it. He took me out to his beach house and had this whole romantic set up for us like I wanted to have sex with him by choice. I refused to let him do that to me again. I couldn't let him do it to me again, I just couldn't." She sobbed.

"It's okay, Cady," I said and rubbed her back to try to calm her.

"No, it's not okay. I killed him, Tehani, and then I cleaned up my mess and set his house on fire so there would be absolutely no evidence. I didn't even know that I was capable of murder until that night. I'm a terrible person."

"No, that motherfucker got exactly what the fuck he deserved! Fuck him for real and if I could I would go spit on his dead fucking body for doing something like that to you. You have no reason to feel bad about what you done, none at all."

"I should have called the police that night. I shouldn't have set his house on fire and ran. My mother only lived ten minutes away from where everything happened. I walked all the way to her house and let myself in with her key. I showered and then changed my clothes because I always left clothes at her house. After that I went back outside and knocked on her front door like nothing had happened. She didn't even know that I had already been inside because she was sleep until I started banging on her door and ringing the doorbell repeatedly. I told her that was me leaving for a little bit and that's when I ended up here."

"Why didn't you just tell your boyfriend so he could help you? I don't get it, wait a minute," I said as I snapped my fingers like a lightbulb had lit up over my head. "The baby isn't his is it? It's the guy who raped you baby," I said, putting two and two together and she nodded her head before speaking again.

"Tee, I couldn't tell my boyfriend because he would have never believed me. He was already very abusive before any of this ever happened. The abuse only had stopped once I became pregnant."

"But why wouldn't he have believed you?"

"Because… it was his brother who done it," she revealed and my mouth damn near hit the floor.

KNOCK! KNOCK! KNOCK! KNOCK!

"Cadence, you can NOT go back to California."

"I have to. Kill is already here, and I told him I would go. I really like him, and he seems to like me, even while I'm pregnant. I can't bail on him and I can't tell him about any of this either. Please go answer the door while I clean myself up and don't say a word to him about any of this. I'll be alright with him with me. I just need to do this and get my doctor's office to fax my information to a doctor's office here. Once we come back I'm never going to California again."

KNOCK! KNOCK! KNOCK!

"Fuck that doctor's office! Call them over the phone and tell them to fax that shit. What if your baby father sees you?"

"He doesn't know about any of this, remember? All he know is that I left him, and I can easily blame that on the abuse if I do happen to see him. Plus Kill won't let him hurt a hair on my head. He's already said that he will keep me safe. Hopefully he can get all of his business handled there today and then tonight I can make up some lame excuse about why I need to get back to Florida. I have to see my mother and tell her what's going on in person. Otherwise she won't understand why I have decided to move here. I can trust her and my father. I mean only if that's okay with you?" she looked at me and asked and then her phone started to ring.

"Of course that's okay with me. I'm just worried about you going back, but I can tell you've made up your mind. Still, the only reason I'm even going to allow you to walk out of this door is because I know that you're going with Kill and he will protect you with his life. Just please be careful and come back as soon as you can," I reluctantly said.

"Thanks so much for understanding. I know I should have told you sooner, but I was afraid that you wouldn't want me around once you knew the truth."

"Girl, do you know who you're talking to? I haven't killed anyone, but I dibble and dabble in some shit. I'll tell you about it once you get back. Go get yourself cleaned up and I will go let Kill in before he kicks my damn door down or some shit." She nodded her head and then got off the bed to go to the bathroom. "One more thing," I said as I walked out of the room behind her.

"What?" she looked back and questioned.

"You have to tell Kill about all of this. It's only right if you plan on getting in a relationship with him."

"I will, but not now." I nodded my head and then headed toward the door after yelling that I was coming. Kill was still banging on it like he was the damn police. "Damn, calm down," I snatched the door open and said.

"What the hell took so long? Is Cadence ready?"

"Yeah, she's in the bathroom and I was in my room. I didn't hear you knocking at first my bad."

"It's cool, where is her bag? I'm going to go ahead and take it to the car."

"I'll get it for you." I walked back down the hall and went back into Cadence's room to get her bag.

Once I had it I rolled it out to the front door where Kill was still standing. He took her bag from me and then turned around to go put it in his car. Cadence finally came out of the bathroom and walked up beside me. I hugged her tightly and made her promise me that she would be careful and text me as soon as they landed. After she done that she walked out and I closed the front door behind her. I went straight to the kitchen and poured myself a shot. After hearing some news like that I needed one. I didn't care how early it was, it was five in the evening some damn where.

I knew Cadence was hiding something from me, but I would have never expected no shit like that. If the motherfucker who raped her wasn't already dead I would go and kill him myself. Hell I really wanted to go and kill her ex-boyfriend for him beating on her. I would have never expected that she had gone through so much. I was glad that she was here with me now and would be moving here for good. I would kill anybody dead before I ever allowed them to hurt her again. She had always been such a sweet girl and she didn't deserve any of that.

I heard my phone ringing in my room, so I quickly took another shot and rushed to answer it just in case it was Keef's ass. When I got to my phone I saw that it was Andrea and not Keef. I quickly pressed the button to answer because it was only a little past five now. Andrea never got up this early and I knew right away that something had to be wrong.

"Hello?"

"Tehani, where are you?" she asked, and I could tell she had been crying.

"I'm at home. Why, what's going on?"

"I need you to get here now, I'm going to send you the address to the motel I'm at."

"Motel! Drea, what are you doing at a motel?"

"Just please hurry and I will explain everything when you get here."

"Okay, I'm on the way!"

Andrea

I hung the phone up from with Tehani and dropped my head in my hands. These last few days of my life had been a complete mess. I ended up having to leave my apartment. There was no way in hell we we're going to be able to stay in that apartment after everything that had gone down. The night after the drugs disappeared I went to work the next morning like nothing had happened.

The whole time while I was at work Boston kept blowing my phone up. I was scheduled to deliver the drugs to him the first thing that next morning. When I didn't show up he wouldn't stop calling. It got so bad that I had to leave work earlier than usual. As soon as I had left I went and got Marsha out of school and we went back to our place and packed our things before coming to the hotel that we was at now.

We had been here for a few days and I was paranoid out of my mind. I hadn't been to work all week and I knew I couldn't even afford to be missing the days that I was missing. I was sleeping this morning when my phone dinging back to back woke me up out of my sleep. Once I grabbed my phone and read the threatening messages that Boston had been sending me I called Tehani. If anyone knew what to do in this situation it would be her. I didn't have long to make a move because I was already out of money after getting this room for a few days. I literally had to check out at eleven this morning and I didn't know what I was going to do next.

"What the hell is going on with you? You have been acting weird since someone stole those bags out of your closet. Not only that but you have us staying in this busted ass motel. Yet you won't tell me shit. This is a bunch of bullshit and I want to go home!" Marsha yelled. She had been eyeing me for the last couple of minutes, but I had tried to ignore her.

I jumped up from the bed and walked over to where she was standing at. Before I knew it I had pushed her up against the wall and my hand went straight to her throat. With everything that was going on I was stressed the fuck out. All I wanted was a better life for both of us. I had just made some fucked up decisions that led us to the situation we was in now.

"Drugs were in those fucking bags you little, Punta! Now I have no way of selling the drugs and getting us the fuck out of here like I had planned to do. A lot of shit is going on that you don't even know about. Don't say shit else to me, okay?" I asked, looking at her like I had been possessed.

"Get the fuck off of me. What dumbass brings drugs to their own house anyway. That's stupid as shit. I swear I should have been born first because you're older and make way more mistakes than me! If you're scared say you're scared, but none of this have shit to do with me. I'm going to get in the shower and get ready for school." She pushed me away from her and then walked away cussing me out in Spanish.

Although I wanted to snatch her up again I just allowed her to go into the bathroom. Putting my hands on her wasn't going to solve the problems that I had. I went back over to the bed and sat down to wait for Tehani. About forty-five minutes later Marsha was getting ready to walk out of the door and as she was walking out Tehani was coming in.

"I got here as quick as I could. What's going on are you alright?" she asked, looking all around the raggedy motel room.

"Tee, I fucked up bad this time. I have really messed the fuck up and now Boston and his homeboys are going to kill me."

"What did you do, Drea?"

"I took some drugs that I was supposed to be delivering to Boston. The only thing is, when I took the drugs they ended up getting stolen the same night. I had plans to sell the drugs and get me and Marsha somewhere nice to stay. I only took the drugs because the guy said I was fired from making deliveries. I had plans for my future with the money I was expecting to keep bringing in from that. He fucked me over, so I fucked them over only to get fucked over and now I don't know what to do. They are going to kill me you already know how they get down. Boston just texted me not too long ago and said those exact words."

"Okay calm down. Let me call Jaydon and see exactly what's going on."

"Are you crazy? We can't fucking call him he is going to tell them where I am."

"You really doubt my pussy powers huh? I'm calling him and he's going to tell us what he knows. We will help you from there. Trust me I got that boy so sprung he will do anything I say."

"I only hope you right because if this backfire you're going to get me fucking killed." I sighed.

"I'm not going to get you killed. Now hush up while I call him," she said, and I just nodded my head. I could only hope that she knew what she was doing because my life was in jeopardy and one wrong move could cost me.

An hour passed by before we heard a loud knock at the motel's room door. I looked at Tehani and she gave me a reassuring look before going over to the curtains in the room. She peeked out them and then went and snatched the door open. Jaydon swaggered in and looked all around my motel room in disgust. I couldn't stand motherfuckers like him because they was always so quick to look down on the next person's situation. If he had a problem with it he could kiss my ass because I had more important shit to worry about.

"You know you fucked up right and Tehani what the hell is going on?" Was the first words to leave Jaydon's mouth.

"You can go. I know I fucked up but that's not why the fuck we called you over here."

"Alright, y'all chill out." Tehani closed the motel's room door back and then went to sit in the chair she had been sitting in.

"I'm not about to chill out. I just talked to Boston yesterday and he told me about your homegirl not showing the fuck up with our drugs. Kill is gone out of town for the weekend but when he comes back he expects this shit to be handled. Boston is looking all over for yo' ass and I don't see why I shouldn't call him and tell him I found you. Where the fuck are our drugs!"

"Tee, what the fuck did I tell you! This is why I didn't want you to call him," I snapped, not believing my ears.

"Jaydon, shut the fuck up. You're not calling nobody and telling them shit. I called you because I wanted to know what you knew."

"All I know is that your homegirl is dead! You called me over here and was playing it like we was about to link up. I wasn't expecting this shit."

"Because if I told you why I really wanted you to meet me here you wouldn't have come."

"You damn right! The only help I got for your girl is advice. Give us our shit and we will forget this even happened. That's my advice to your ass now what you do next is on you."

"I don't have the fucking drugs! If I had them don't you think I would have delivered them?" I asked. I knew I was lying but it was best to just play it cool.

"That's bullshit and we both know it. The drugs weren't magically stolen. You had been making the deliveries before this and nothing ever happened. Which I don't even know why that nigga had you picking up our shit. That was stupid on his fucking part. Y'all gone mess around and get everybody killed. Oh, and I'm calling Boston and telling him I found your ass too," Jaydon said and then turned to leave out.

"I don't think so," I said making everyone whip around and look at me.

"Drea, what the fuck are you doing?" Tehani questioned, eyes wide and on the gun I had pointed straight at Jaydon's head.

I don't know what made me do it, but I was desperate for a way out. I told Tehani before she invited him over that he wasn't going to help us. She wasn't even giving him no pussy so I knew he couldn't be trusted. Maybe I should have left her out of it from the get, but I was already in a hole. After the move I was about to pull I knew I would only be in an even deeper one but at this point it was do or die and I didn't plan to die. **POW!**

Cadence

Kill and I was just pulling out of the airport parking lot. We had landed about an hour ago, but it took us that long just to get our bags and things and get situated before we could leave. Now we were heading to my doctor's office and I felt nauseous in the passenger seat as I tried to instruct Kill where to go. My palms were sweaty, and my heartbeat was faster than usual. I just knew that Kill could hear it beating in my chest sitting next to me. He didn't say anything or seemed to notice my uneasiness though, so I figured I was doing a pretty good job of controlling myself on the outside. But on the inside, it was a whole different story.

I honestly wanted to tell Kill to turn around and take me back to the airport so I could take the first plane back out. Even my baby girl was going haywire in my stomach as if she knew we were in dangerous territory. I couldn't quite put my finger on it, but something just felt so wrong. I tried to chalk it up to just be my nerves because I hadn't been home since that awful night. I would never forget that night. It had definitely been the worst night of my entire life. I had held on to my truth for as long as I could, but finally telling someone about that night made me feel a little better.

I had always been very cool with Lennox's brother Lance. When I was into it with Lennox I could go to Lance and he would make me feel better by sitting and talking with me. Over the last six years of my relationship with Lennox, Lance and I had created a genuine friendship. After a while I had even started to look at him as if he was my brother. Lennox and I had never got married or anything, but Lance was truly a brother to me, or so I thought.

It wasn't until six months ago when things got crazy, but before that I would have never seen it coming. While I thought I was building a genuine bond with him he was catching feelings for me. I felt so stupid when I thought back to the times we would hang out. All of the signs were there, but I had read them wrong or just brushed them off to be nothing at the time. The first night he raped me he had been drinking and made a bold advance at me that I quickly turned down. Well, it turned out that he was more like his brother than I had thought, if not worse. He took what he wanted from me and didn't think twice about it.

I cried for days trying to make it all make sense. I didn't understand how he could go from so sweet to so cruel after all of those years of us building a friendship. At first I told myself that he was drunk, and he didn't know what he was doing. Things only got more complicated when I realized I was pregnant. Lennox and I didn't have sex often but for some strange reason he wanted to have sex with me about a week after I had been raped by his brother.

It was a hard thing to do but I did it anyway. What was I going to tell him? No, we can't have sex right now because your brother just raped me last week. I think not, that shit wouldn't have gone well at all. Mainly because I knew he wouldn't believe me, which is why I kept it to myself to begin with. He would often accuse us of having something going on and I would tell him continuously that it wasn't anything like that. So I knew if I told him I had been raped he would have put all the blame on me. Then, he probably would have beaten my baby out of me himself. It just wasn't something I was willing to go through if I could avoid it and keep the truth to myself.

Now was I a hundred percent sure that my baby was Lance's and not Lennox's? No I wasn't, but there was this gut feeling I had. I just knew the baby wasn't Lennox's. As long as we had been having sex I had never been impregnated by him. He had even told me a few times himself that he didn't think it was possible for him to have kids.

Yet, he never had that suspicion verified. Aside from all of that my due date added up to when I was raped and not when Lennox and I had sex a week after. There was still a slim chance that the baby could very well be Lennox's, but I knew better. I was just glad that I was able to pin the baby on him once we figured out I was pregnant. I had been a nervous wreck since that day and when Lance tried to take advantage of me that second time I completely lost it.

I couldn't let him do it a second time and I ended up stabbing him to death. I was so scared that someone would know that it was me who had done it that I set his beach house on fire to get rid of all of the evidence. After that I fled and now here I was back in the same city that had cost me so much turmoil. I knew I shouldn't have gone to his beach house with him that night to start with, but he had left me with no choice. It was either I could go with him or he would tell his brother that I was having his baby.

Since I knew all of the blame would be put on me, I went. Lennox was out working late as usual and I convinced myself that Lance just wanted to apologize in private. Well, it was a whole different story when I got there and saw the romantic set up he had for us. That's when I realized he wasn't sorry at all, but he truly wanted me for himself. All those times he would tell me that Lennox didn't deserve me was only because he felt like he did. I had been through hell with that family and it was nothing short of a miracle that I was even able to feel secure with another man.

"Are you alright?" I heard Kill ask next to me, snapping me out of my thoughts.

"Yes, I'm fine. What makes you ask that?"

"You're gripping the door handle hard as shit right now."

"I'm sorry." I slowly let the door handle go.

"It's cool."

"Make this turn coming up. I meant to tell you to turn back there."

"Aight."

"What are we doing after we leave the doctor's office?" I questioned, trying to take the focus off of myself.

"We're going to get you and the baby something to eat. I know y'all have to be starving by now."

"Actually, I am. I didn't even think about it until you said something."

"That's that pregnancy brain."

"Oh yeah, I forgot you're an expert on pregnant women." I joked. "I didn't even need to see the doctor with you around."

"You was gone see the doctor, regardless."

"Okay, my bad." I grew quiet for a few minutes.

It amazed me how he took my pregnancy so serious. I took it serious too, but I didn't think it was a crime to joke about it. I guess if I had gone through what he had been through I would feel the same. I reached over and lightly rubbed his arm and I saw his face relax a little. He was still a big mystery to me, but I guess he could say the same about me. I told him the office was coming up on the right and he slowed down to make the turn.

We turned into the office and I was brought back to my reality. I scanned the parking lot to see if I saw Lennox's car anywhere. When I didn't I was able to relax a little again. Kill parked as close as he could to the door and then hopped out and jogged around the car to open my door and help me out. Once I was out he slammed my door shut and then placed his hand on my back to guide me to the door. We walked in and I went to the front desk to get checked in. I wanted to get in and out as quickly as possible.

If it was one place that Lennox would be able to find me it would be here. That's why I hadn't even attempted to make my previous appointments. He didn't know I was coming back to town though, so I tried not to worry too much. I just hoped that my mother had kept her mouth closed. Since he was going over there daily I knew I wouldn't be able to go to her house to see her. Hopefully she would be able to come out and meet me somewhere so we could talk.

I had only been sitting down for about ten minutes when the doctor walked out and called me back. Kill looked at me and asked if I wanted him to come back with me. I told him I would be fine and then followed the doctor out of the waiting area. I didn't want to make it hard on Kill by making him sit through my ultrasound and things. He was such a good guy and I found myself wanting to be his more and more every day. With the situation I had going on it seemed damn near impossible.

I kept telling myself to just be truthful with him and he would understand, but deep down inside I felt like if he knew I had been raped he wouldn't want to be with me. It made me feel dirty and like I wasn't worthy of a good man. That may not have been true, but I couldn't help but to feel like it was. The doctor had an uneasy look on his face from the moment he saw me sitting with Kill. I didn't know what that was all about. I just figured he felt some type of way about seeing me with Kill since he was so used to seeing me and Lennox together. I wanted to explain that me and Kill was just friends, but I didn't even bother.

"Go ahead inside and get changed. I'll uhm… be back shortly."

"Okay." I nodded my head and then walked into the room to change out of my clothes and put on the gown he had given me.

Before I could even finish getting undressed my door was flying open. I thought that was rude as hell because the doctor hadn't knocked or anything. I turned around to see what was going on and when I did I dropped my phone on the floor. I couldn't make a sound or even move as the person walked in and closed the door behind them.

"Put your fucking shirt back on now!" Lennox barked and I started to tremble.

"What…what are you doing here?"

"Don't ask me any fucking questions, Cade. Put your shirt on and do what the fuck I say or I'm going to kill your ass in this doctor's office. You thought you could run away from me? Is that what it was? I have been going crazy without you and then I get here and you're perfectly fucking fine. Do you know how big of a slap that is in the face? Do you!" he yelled, and I quickly shook my head no.

"Did my mother tell you I was going to be here today?" I stupidly asked.

"Nah, she didn't have to tell me shit. The bitch is a liar just like you and you're lucky she's not dead. Now put your shirt on and come on before the doctor comes back in."

"No, I'm not going anywhere with you." I started to cry. I knew this shit would happen. I just knew it would. I instantly started to regret not letting Kill come back with me, but I was only trying to prevent him from going into an emotional slump. I looked at Lennox and prepared myself to scream as loud as I could. I couldn't go anywhere with him. I just knew he was going to kill me from the look in his eyes. He was going to beat me worse than he ever had before.

"Don't you even fucking think about it," he said and then lifted up his shirt to reveal the gun that was on his side. "I'm not going to ask you anymore to put your shirt on, Cadence," Lennox said with a sinister look on his face. I done as I was told, and he smiled. "Good girl," he said before roughly grabbing me by the arm. "Now let's go."

Killian

Cadence had just been called to the back when a dark skinned dude with a beard walked in and marched straight to the front desk. He was dressed in a green button up shirt with a tie to match and a pair of kakis. I scrunched up my nose at the nigga because who the fucked dressed like that to come to the doctor's office? He didn't even look my way when he had walked in, but I knew something was wrong when I heard him ask for Cadence. I jumped up to go over to the desk, but they had escorted him to the back so quickly that I didn't have time to get to him.

"I need to get to the back to check on Cadence," I said to the receptionist who had started doing something on the computer.

"I'm sorry sir, who are you?"

"I'm Cadence's boyfriend," I said, knowing they wouldn't let me in the back any other way. Plus, I had every intention of becoming that, so I wasn't telling a lie.

"No, her boyfriend who is her child's father just came and asked for her. I had someone to escort him to the room she was in. I don't know who you are or what you're doing, but we can't let you back there."

"What the fuck! I know you just seen me walk in here with her!" I yelled. I was still trying to keep my cool because I didn't want to get kicked out, but the receptionist was going to make me do something real fucking stupid.

"Sir, I saw you walk in here with her, but I've never seen you around here before. If she wanted you in the back with her she would have asked you to come when she went back. The child's father is in the back now and to prevent any problems I'm not going to be able to let you back there. You need to take a seat and wait for her to come back out." That was all she said before going back to tapping at the keys on her computer.

I was about to lose my fucking cool when my phone started ringing in my pocket. I thought it could have been Cadence, so I pulled it out right away and answered it, not paying any attention at all to the name on the screen.

"Where the fuck are you!" a girl screamed into the phone.

"Who the hell is this?" I questioned and pulled my phone away from my ear to look at the screen. When I saw the name I began to see red. This couldn't be right.

"It's Tyra. I was released today, and I've been knocking on your door for the last thirty minutes. Where are you at? We really need to talk."

How the fuck could this be happening and who the hell had let my baby's murderer out of jail? This shit was too much for me right now, especially with everything that was going on. My chest started to ache and just the sound of her voice alone made me want to strangle her. Nigga's went to jail longer for a drug charge and now somehow…some way… a murderer had been let out on the streets. It wasn't making any fucking sense. Instead of answering her I hung the phone up and ran straight to the back. Fuck what that receptionist was talking about. I needed to get to Cadence.

"Sir! Someone call security!" I heard her yell as I started busting into all of the rooms in the back in search of Cadence.

When I got to the last room on the left the door was already open, but no one was inside. I was about to walk away but that's when I spotted Cadence's phone on the floor. I rushed in to pick it up. That bastard had her, but he was in for one hell of a fight. I still didn't know her backstory with him and at this point it didn't matter. He had to be who she was running from all of this time and I had basically brought her straight to him.

"Fuck!" I yelled before running out of the room and back out to the waiting area.

Once I was in the waiting area I ran straight outside to my car. When I did I saw a car damn near on two wheels trying to get away. That had to be them, but I wasn't sure because the tint on the windows was so dark. I figured he had snuck her out the back and took off. He could run but he couldn't fucking hide. I was officially out for blood and anyone who got in my way was going to die. I wasn't called Kill because it was short for Killian, but because it was what I was known for doing, and now I had a point to prove and a girl to save. Everything was cool until you played with a boss because one thing I didn't do was play. Once I was played with shit was bound to get ugly and it was only up from here.

To Be Continued…

Lennox

"Who was that, who the fuck was that?" I shouted as I sped out of the parking lot of the doctor's office.

"I don't know." Cadence cried, pissing me off even more than I already was. She didn't have shit to be crying about. At least not yet she didn't anyway.

"So you don't know who the nigga with the Florida license plate at YOUR doctor's office was? Funny," I said stepping on the gas.

"I said I don't know who he is, Lenny," she insisted.

"Then why the fuck is he following us?"

I stepped on the gas and then made a sharp turn to the left. I drove to the end of the street and then made another sharp turn. When I looked in the rearview mirror I didn't see him behind us anymore, so I assumed I had lost him. Yet, that didn't stop me from speeding and making a few more unnecessary turns to make sure I had really lost the motherfucker.

"Please slow down!"

"Why the fuck should I! Tell me why I shouldn't just kill us both right now! I know you were in Florida. At first I thought you had just ran off to get away from me, but now I see you ran the fuck off to be with a nigga!"

"That's not true."

"It is true!"

"It's not!"

"Well tell me the fucking truth because shit isn't making sense! On top of all of this my brother is fucking dead!"

"Lance is dead?" she had the fucking nerve to gasp, but the look on her face told me everything I needed to know… she knew something.

"You both go missing around the same time and then when he's found he's dead and you're in a whole different state with another nigga. How fucking ironic is that!"

"Lennox, I swear to god I don't know what happened to Lance. I left to clear my head. You know we were going through so much. I just needed time away." She sniffed.

"Stop it with your fucking tears. You know I don't give a shit about you crying. Now tell me who the fuck that guy was back there!"

"I told you I didn't—"

Wham! I pushed her head up against the glass window. When I looked over she hadn't passed out or anything, but there was blood dripping down her face from where her forehead had met the glass.

"Now stop lying and tell me who the fuck he is."

"He's just a friend I met while I was visiting my other friend."

"Then why the fuck is he here with you in California? Let me guess, he's your new boyfriend?"

"Boyfriend, do you see me?" she asked, barely above a whisper.

"Obviously he doesn't give a shit about you being pregnant if he's flying you out to doctor appointments and shit. I'm going to get the truth out of you one way or another. So enjoy this ride bitch, because it just might be the last one you take!"

I sped the remainder of the way to our home that we once shared together. It had been so lonely over the last month. I couldn't understand why the fuck Cadence would leave just to get away from me. Once she became pregnant with my baby the ass whooping's had stopped, but she could kiss that advantage away now. I was going to beat her ass black and blue.

As soon as I parked the car I hopped out and walked around to her side. I snatched her door open and grabbed her by the hair as hard as I could. I didn't even give her the chance to step out of the car before pulling her out and dragging her ass all the way to our front door. The only thing she kept hollering about was the baby, but I didn't give a shit about that. My brother was dead, and she was back. I was going to get the answers I wanted, or my parents weren't going to be the only ones planning a funeral. She hadn't seen anything… yet.

STAY CONNECTED

Reader's Group
Kai'or Elle's Reading Group
Email
kaiorelle@gmail.com

facebook.com/kaior.elle.7

Royalty Publishing House is now accepting manuscripts from aspiring or experienced urban romance authors!

WHAT MAY PLACE YOU ABOVE THE REST:

Heroes who are the ultimate book bae: strong-willed, maybe a little rough around the edges but willing to risk it all for the woman he loves.

Heroines who are the ultimate match: the girl next door type, not perfect - has her faults but is still a decent person. One who is willing to risk it all for the man she loves.

The rest is up to you! Just be creative, think out of the box, keep it sexy and intriguing!

If you'd like to join the Royal family, send us the first 15K words (60 pages) of your completed manuscript to submissions@royaltypublishing-house.com

LIKE OUR PAGE!

ROYALTY
PUBLISHING HOUSE

Be sure to LIKE our Royalty Publishing House page on Facebook!